By the Same Author

THE KINGDOM OF FANES

Amanda Prantera

BLOOMSBURY

First published 1995
Copyright © 1995 by Amanda Prantera
The moral right of the author has been asserted
Bloomsbury Publishing Plc, 2 Soho Square, London W1V 6HB

A CIP catalogue record for this book is available
from the British Library

ISBN 0 7475 20038

Typeset by
Hewer Text Composition Services, Edinburgh
Printed in Great Britain by
WBC Ltd, Bridgend, South Wales

Drawings by Connie Prantera

For Tegan

Opening Note to Readers. Whoever, Wherever and Whenever They May Be

Writing of my own free will, without a Shaman or a Commander or some other fusspot standing over me hissing with impatience, driving me on, is something I haven't done for ages. And the same goes for drawing. I set about doing both these things now for the plain reason that there is nothing else here for me to do. Needlework gets on my nerves (the light isn't good enough anyway); singing or music-making of any kind disturbs the others. I have tried a little light carpentry and wood-carving but that too creates a disturbance, particularly when the wood is hard and I get cross and clumsy and start dropping things. Nobody has complained – they wouldn't dare – but I see the older ones turning over and eyeing me blearily and burying their heads deeper in their bedding in search of silence, and I can hear them thinking, Fidgety old fool, why on earth did we go and saddle ourselves with her? Should have left her to the ravens. *They'd* have taught her how to spend a quiet winter and no mistake.

So I must make do with pen and inks and brushes, and even these I have to handle carefully. I respect these people, you see, and that entails respecting their time-table. There is however another reason, a less selfish reason, for this record or chronicle or whatever these pages may turn out to be, and that is to leave behind me a kind of measuring-rod or touchstone of the truth for future generations. Wise though my companions are in many ways, I am not, very definitely not, living among scholars. Books they love, particularly ones with pictures in them, and I am sure any writings and drawings I leave them will be guarded like treasures, even by the non-readers, but they won't open them often for fear of spoiling them, and the events of these recent years will most likely be passed on to newcomers the way they always have been: by means of stories, told by the best but not always most truthful narrator. Only a few fortnights ago, for example, just by way of a test I asked Etti, one of the brightest of my younger listeners, to repeat to me the story I had told her about the treachery of the False Regent, and although she got most of it right I noticed to my dismay that she called him throughout not the False Regent but the Falzarego and seemed to have got it into her head (perhaps on account of his size, which I admit I may have overdone a bit – and why not, the vile old dumpling?) that he was not a real person at all but a mountain.

If such a slide in meaning is possible after just one telling, what will happen, I ask myself, after five, or ten, or a hundred? Will we all of us – Dolasilla, Lujanta, me, Lois, Ey de Net, Sonia, Tilly and the others – be turned into peaks and valleys, our struggles into thunderstorms, our defeats into landslides? Will our names be twisted beyond recognition to suit the sing-song language – all ups and downs, rather like a mountain range itself? No doubt they will, and this is therefore my second reason for writing: not only to help me while away these long stretches of unmarked, undivided time, but in order to leave behind me when I die a reliable, lasting account of what happened, so that when the stories get out of hand and even the littlest children have difficulty believing them, someone can shift away the stone from the hidey-hole where all the precious possessions are kept and burrow in the darkness and fish out these papers and say, 'Wait, now, that sounds a bit much – a mountain belching! Let's have a look in the old woman's book and see what really happened. Let's turn to the picture of this Falzarego or whatever it was called and see what it looked like. Here we are, it was a he, see, not an it. It was a person; that is, *he* was a person. Here he is on page 12 with his beard and bulgy midriff and freckled head and all.'

Another thing I would like to do to lower the risk of muddles and misunderstandings, is to be able to mark my pages in such a way that future readers will know immediately in which times the events I describe took place. But since years do not have names or numbers, this is more or less impossible. (I did think of asking Etti to scratch a cross on the cover of the papers at the beginning of each winter, and to instruct her children to do the same, and the children of her children and so on; but paper reserves are getting low now that we use so much of it for lessons, and there is the danger that the pages would end up as playthings, to be scribbled on just for the fun of it, and that wouldn't do at all.)

Over the question of the exact spot where the events took place, on the other hand, no problems should arise. The world may be, as Zeno said, much larger than we in these parts think it is, and the papers may be moved from hiding place to hiding place as the group itself is obliged to move, but whoever finds them in the end has only to raise their head to the horizon and pick out the ridge of the Great White Saddle, the skew-set cap of Putia, the Marbleblock, the knob of the Tofana with the

Crystal Fangs beyond it, to recognize the site straight away. However big the world is, however far you ride, there can't be another skyline such as this one, that's for certain. And now to business.

CHAPTER ONE

My Beloved Prison

I was brought up to think of myself as someone very special, and to think that everybody else thought me special too. (Which they did, of course, but not for the reasons I imagined.) This had a bad effect on me at first, and I am afraid that right up to the day of my twelfth birthday I was – not always, but often – hasty and vain and wilful, and careless of other people's feelings. I had twelve ponies to ride – one for every day of the fortnight almost – and when I had finished my ride for the day I would leap off the saddle and leave the pony with one of the stable boys, not bothering even to loosen the girth: the boy would see to that, that was what he was there for. I never cleaned my tack, didn't even know that it needed cleaning, never went near the stables except to pat the ponies' heads over the top of the doors, never picked up a curry comb or carried a bucket or did anything useful at all.

And this is only one example. I could give you others. My clothes, for instance: not only did I not have to fold them up or put them away in the chests, I didn't even have to fasten them round me or unfasten them when I undressed. All I had to do was hold out my arms so that Nurse could get to the back of me, and wait while she buttoned me up. Or unbuttoned me, as was the case. And even then I am ashamed to say I sometimes grumbled at her for her slowness. I didn't have to wash myself, I didn't have to brush my own hair, and (believe it or not) I didn't really, not unless I chose to, have to wipe my own bottom after I had been on the squat-pail. 'Quite the little princess aren't we?' Nurse used to say when I called her to carry out this not very pleasant task. But she said it quietly, well out of my mother's hearing, because that of course was exactly what I was: a princess. *The* princess, the one and only, the solitary little peg on which so many people's hopes and futures hung.

Now that I am old myself – far older than they ever were, and in a much trickier position as far as politics are concerned – I can understand the way my parents felt, and why they treated me as they did. Not only as a worried mother and father, but as a worried King and Queen, as worried leaders of a threatened and worried people, they were terrified of losing me, terrified of doing something wrong which would result in my injury or dis-figurement or, worse still, death. For this reason they spoilt me, and at the same time treated me rather like a prisoner – a very pampered prisoner, but a prisoner nonetheless.

My bedroom was in the West Keep, above the Armoury where the weapons are stored. *Were* stored. I was never allowed to go near the window alone, even though there were wooden bars on it thick as martens' tails: that was the way my brother had met his end, crawling out onto the ledge with a pair of home-made wings on his back, trying to fly like an eagle. I missed this brother I never knew, although by all accounts he was a cocksure little character, even more full of himself than I was. Must have been, come to think of it, or he wouldn't have held himself capable of flying. But still, cocksure or not, I missed him, and for a lot of reasons.

I was never allowed to ride alone either, or to go out for walks alone, or to splash around in the moat with the other children when it was hot, or to slide down the mountainside with them on the soldiers' shields when it was cold. (I'm not sure they would have wanted me to either – the other children, I mean: I was so used to giving orders and getting my own way in everything I would have probably spoiled their games for them, bossed them around and changed all the rules and whatnot.) When I woke up in the morning Nurse was there already, with a flannel in one hand to wash my face for me, and a tray with my breakfast on it in the other. Milk and cheese and fruit, and special soft bread, when everybody else, even my father, had to make do with hard. After breakfast she would call for Sonia, the nursemaid, and together they would dress me: Sonia doing all the tiresome things that called for bending, like rummaging in the chests, and lacing my shoes, and picking up the clothes I cast aside (because, yes, I was fussy about what I wore), and Nurse, unable to vent her anger on me, venting it on Sonia instead, 'Blockhead! Clumsy-paws! Sister to a badger! Be quick with those bows, or we'll be here till kingdom come.' Poor little Sonia, I wish I had been kinder to her then, paid more attention to her. I thought of her (if I thought of her at all) as a grown-up worker, but she was in fact not much older than I was myself. I remember noticing her hands, though, and feeling sorry for her on this account: under the fur they were always red.

When I was dressed and ready, Lois would be called to take me to my parents, and then on to the schoolroom. He was a cousin of Sonia's, of the same patient, uncomplaining stock, and it was his task to accompany me everywhere I went, close and silent like a shadow. (In the winter his job would be taken over by a young woman called Tecla, a Fane like myself, who sulked a lot and

thought the assignment vastly beneath her dignity.)
He wasn't supposed to speak to me or make any
comment on what I did, unless it was something
dangerous or forbidden, in which case he was
allowed to say the single word 'No' and then
ask my pardon for his boldness in addressing me.
It was rather a silly arrangement but we both of us
stuck by it, being too silly ourselves, I suppose, to
think up a different one.

We would go down the winding wooden stairs,
through the Armoury where the soldiers were busy
burnishing their arrowheads or whatever it was
they did to them in those days, across the courtyard
and into the kitchen, where my mother would be
sitting in her special wool-padded seat, looking
deathly bored, pretending to count things. 'Three
hundred and twenty-five,' she would sigh in the
direction of the sack of nuts or prunes or apples that
was being passed under her nose for her inspection,
'Three hundred and twenty-six . . . Ah, there you
are, Alexa. Good, good. Run along now or you'll
be late . . . Three hundred and twenty-seven,
three hundred and twenty-eight, three hundred
and twenty – Oh, zitherstrings! where was I? –
three hundred and twenty-wretched-nine.' Sometimes, as Lois and I walked away, I would hear her
muddling up the sequence with a mischievous
tone in her voice, or else inventing numbers out
of her head, 'Stickely-hive, Sedentary-flea, Seden-
tary-boar.' It used to embarrass me slightly on

account of the kitchen workers who took the whole business very seriously, but I didn't suppose it mattered much: after all, they were only Salvans like Sonia and Lois and none of them could count.

My father, already busy with his counsellors in the Thinking Chamber at this time of the morning, would pay a little more attention to me. I think he was glad of an excuse to take his heavy decision-maker's head-dress off and put aside his papers: he too needed someone standing over him breathing down his neck before he would do any desk work, and his fingers, I remember, were always badly ink-stained, like a beginner's. So was his moustache, because that was where he lodged his pen. 'Off to your lessons, Alexa?' he would ask, never waiting for a reply. 'That's the spirit. Learning! Wonderful stuff! The key to the world, I always say, you can't get enough of it. And what has Zeno got in store for my little Alexa today, eh? Pot-hooks? Curlicues? Flourishes? Links? Mind you pay attention to him, precious, and don't make him angry. Good teachers are worth their weight in pig bristles nowadays.' Then, after one or two more perfunctory questions about whether I was eating properly and keeping out of trouble, he would hold out his inky hand for me to kiss (or, if he was in an affectionate mood, indicate a spot on his cheek just above his inky whiskers), signal to his page to replace the head-dress, and disappear under the cascade of fur and chamois' horns. The

12

important thing, you see, for both my parents, seemed to be not so much to talk to me or listen to me, but just to know that I was there, still alive and breathing.

Having made my curtsey to the strange, hairy-topped figure my father had now become, I would back out of his presence with a slowness that he and the counsellors took for respect – very right and proper in a daughter – but was in fact my way of staving off for as long as possible the dreaded lesson-times with Zeno. Lois would giggle some-times as we made our shuffling, dragging, zig-zag way towards the exit, and I think he knew exactly what I was doing and why, but he never interfered to speed me up. Nor did he try to correct me when, as I nearly always did, I chose an unnecessarily long route to reach the schoolroom. Even when I went up one turret and across the connecting ramparts and down another, and crossed the courtyard twice, and took a detour round by the sheep-pens and through the laundry and over the ice-pits and back via the storerooms where all the items counted by my mother were stored and labelled, he said no 'No's, just tagged along behind, smiling all over his plain, brown, leathery conker of a face.

My father said Zeno as a teacher was worth his weight in pig bristles. Well, if I'd taken the man to market I would have gladly swapped him for the equivalent in hay, perhaps even straw. Not that he wasn't a nice man, mind you. In fact he was a very harmless, very polite, very quiet and gentle man who probably knew all sorts of things besides the reading and writing and reckoning with numbers that he was hired to teach me, but he was so dull, so incredibly, hugely, gigantically dull, that it was almost impossible to listen for longer than a bat's wing-beat to anything he said. He would always use my full title, too, which made his sentences even longer and more predictable. 'Crown Princess Alexa of All the Fanes' he would say each time I entered the schoolroom. 'Good morning, Crown Princess Alexa of All the Fanes. And what, if I may ask, would Crown Princess Alexa of All the Fanes like to set her wits to this morning? Shall it be how to keep a straight margin? Shall it be how to add digits to one another without the use of fingers? Yours is the choice, Princess Alexa of All the Fanes. Speak, and your teacher will comply with your wishes.' It may be, of course, that he was bored himself, and that his politeness had a tinge of sarcasm to it; perhaps the letter of introduction he brought with him was genuine, and he did indeed come from a country where books were as common as doormats and even the chickens knew how to read and write, and his solemn repetition of my title was not politeness at all but a private joke between himself and himself: 'Crown Princess Woollyhead of all the Goats'. But if this was the case, I still don't see why he

14

couldn't have tried to make his lessons more
amusing instead of making them so dreary. If *I*
had to teach a goat for my living, I mean, I would
try to make it fun – both for me and the goat.

Anyway, those were my mornings. Ink and
tedium and splotches, and rows and rows of
never-ending strokes: straight, curved, sloping,
looping; circles, hoops, crossbars, dots and tadpoles. The key to the world, as my father called it.
(And now that I sit here in dimly lit silence with
only my pen for company, I look down at this frail
little instrument in my hands and think gratefully
that he was right: it *is* a key, and with it I *can* enter
another world.) Afternoons, luckily, were a different matter. Sometimes, if there were storms or
anything, there would be a reading lesson in which
I would be set the task of deciphering some piece
of written material, like my mother's household
lists, or Zeno's famous letter of introduction
(which I knew by heart after a couple of times
although I never said so); but otherwise, in the
normal course of things, the afternoons belonged
to the outdoors, and the woods, and freedom.

Zeno would have to come too, of course,
because it was part of his duties to keep an eye
on me in the afternoons as well as the mornings,
but horses must have been few in the country he
came from (perhaps the ones that there were were
all busy writing), and he was a nervous, clumsy
rider, easy to outdistance or leave behind alto-

gether. He was also either ashamed of this failing, or else simply tactful, because instead of mentioning it to my parents, as I suppose he should have done, he made a pact with me by which we each went our own way and met up on the fringe of the wood afterwards, ready to return to the stables together. What he did in the interval I have no idea: his horse always looked cool and rested, but he himself usually had a funny flushed look about him and he sometimes had trouble climbing back into the saddle, so I have a suspicion he spent the time drinking Schniappa. (Which, if so, would explain why he told no tales.)

With no bodyguard save for Lois, therefore, who followed on foot and was so quiet about it that I often didn't notice him at all, I would be free to go where I liked, for as long as I liked provided I was back before sundown. I would ride up the slopes of what we called the Friendly Mountains – the ones the afternoon sun shone on – and see if I could find strawberries, or cadge a bowl of milk from one of the cowherds. Or else, if I was feeling more daring, I would venture up the paths of the Frowning Mountains, on the opposite side of the valley where the shadows were darker and the trees were thicker, and where wolves were reputed to lurk, waiting for someone or something shorter than themselves to pounce on for their evening meal. Sometimes, in the good season when the days were longer, I would go straight down the valley itself, as far as the broken bridge where the old man lived who did the carving, and dismount and sit with him, and watch him while he worked. It was then, I suppose, that I picked up my taste for carpentry. Funny, how much I learnt, just from watching. I wish other things had come to me in the same painless way.

There was a fourth ride too (or rather a fourth and fifth and a sixth and a goodness-knows-whatth, because once you rode *up* the valley and reached the foot of the real snow-clad mountains the tracks branched off in dozens of different directions: you could go to the green lake, the silver lake, the poppy fields, the Rabbit-woman's hut, almost anywhere in the world you liked), but for some reason I hardly ever went that way. Not because it frightened me – the Frowning Mountains were far more scary – but because it gave me a kind of uncomfortable, lost feeling. Once or twice I got as far as the great frozen waterfall where the valley road stopped and the other tracks split off from it and began to climb, but as I sat there on my pony under the dark jagged shadow cast by the wall of ice, wondering which track to take, I felt so small and foolish and out of place that I was unable to go forward. Lois longed for us to go on, I know he did: somewhere up in those cold white regions was where his home lay, and I could see him sniffing the air with relish as if it was a bowl of delicious soup; the pony too flared its nostrils and pawed at the ground and seemed eager to make the climb. But I felt differently, more as if unseen noses were smelling *me* and not liking what they smelled, and I had to disappoint my two companions and turn round and make straight for home again. It may only have been leaves caught in the ice, or a trick of the light or something, but on one occasion, perhaps it was the first time, perhaps the second, I could have sworn I actually saw a pair of squinty black eyes looking out at me from behind the waterfall. Glaring at me. Warning me off.

What with breakfast and midday meals and rides, and feast days when there weren't any lessons, and evenings spent stretched out in front of the fire with the dogs, playing knucklebones or chequers with an imaginary opponent, my life, although rather solitary and sheltered, was really very happy. A few things I dreaded of course: besides lessons there were sewing sessions with my mother, examinations by the Shaman and the tooth-puller, yearly hair-washes and nit inspections by Nurse, the never-ending Spring Festival when I would have to sit for the whole day on a hard stool at my father's feet, smiling at people as they filed past with their gifts and saying, Dër bel iolan, Dër bel iolan, Dër bel iolan, until my tongue turned into a biscuit. Things like that, I could willingly have done without. But otherwise, right up to the morning – the late morning in fact it was – of my twelfth birthday, when everything changed and myself with it, I wouldn't really have swapped my position for that of anybody else in the entire kingdom. Save possibly the head stable-man, who had no hair and no teeth and no lessons and no mother, and was always among his beloved horses, and seemed to me to lead an altogether perfect life.

CHAPTER TWO

The Real Falzarego

ow that I am old I have developed a good nose for trouble: I can usually smell it before it strikes and do something to try to avoid it. At just turned twelve I was not so practised. (And even if I had been, what could I have done? Run away? Flown out of the window like my brother?)

The business over the hair should have alerted me. It wasn't anywhere near yearly washing time, and yet Nurse woke me early that day, before the sun was up, and began trundling in all the basins and pitchers and stuff that she used for just this purpose. Seven pitchers, two basins, one for clear water, one for soapy, seven slop-pails, an array of combs and cards and scrubbing brushes that made your scalp ache just to look at them. When I started to protest she slapped the flannel over my face smartly and told me to hold it there if I didn't want soap in my eyes. '*Her* orders,' she said. 'Her' in this tone of voice meant my mother. 'Says you've got to look your best. Wants ribbons plaited into it too. All this palaver, and no warning, no thanks. I don't know what the world's coming to, I'm sure. Where has that lazy creature got to? Never here when she's needed. Sonia! Sonia! Sooonia!'

Yes, I should have suspected that something bad, or at any rate out of the ordinary, was on the programme that day. When Sonia arrived her eyes were red, even redder than her hands; she wore a clean white apron with lace on it, much smarter than her usual blue one, and her hair was tied in bunches over her ears, making her look as if she had four of them (four ears, I mean). It too was given a surprise dunking in the last slop-pail when Nurse had finished rinsing mine. 'That'll have to do,' Nurse said as she pulled her out again. 'I'm not tackling the rest, not for all the gold in Aurona.'

I wasn't allowed to choose what I wanted to wear the way I usually did, either, but after my hair had been rubbed and combed and pulled and plaited and tied up and skewered with hair-prongs to Nurse's satisfaction, I was bundled into my stiff red dress with all the embroidery on it that I wore on feast days, and laced tight at the waist. I felt taut and shiny like a sausage.

And stupid like a sausage, I still didn't realize that

I was on my way to table. Lois could have warned me, of course. He knew by then what was going on, he could have broken his silence and warned me. But when I complained to him about this afterwards, he pointed out very sensibly that there would have been no point: when the news is bad and you can do nothing to change it, the later you learn about it the better. Like Sonia after her wetting, he had a funny, scrubbed look about him and his eyes were watery. I put this down to the rain: it was pouring that morning. Nature, as Zeno might have said, had he not been sent on his way already as an unnecessary expense now that his pupil no longer needed him, was mourning the lost happiness of Alexa, Crown Princess of All the Fanes.

The King and Queen my parents, far from mourning, looked contented as cats in the larder, as if by their cunning and stealth they had landed some kind of much contested prize. Which I suppose to their way of thinking they had. Dukes in our parts, with castles and followers and sheep and furniture, and without wives or debts or children or other encumbrances, were very hard to come by. In fact the one now sitting in their throne room as if he owned the place, cleaning the mud off his boots with my mother's best needlework cushion and then smelling at it to make sure it was mud and not something worse, was probably the only one there was.

Now, I dislike unfairness in others, so I must try
to be fair myself and not allow my later judgement
of the man to interfere and make me describe him as
even worse than he was. After all, he is – perhaps, I
am not really sure about this – the father of at least
one of my children, so on this account I owe him a
scrap of loyalty. He was old, for a start. Shockingly
old. In his late twenties, perhaps even early thirties:
my father, no chicken at twenty-five, looked like a
boy beside him. (Unlike mine, the Duke's mother
was not a counter, and she was dead anyway, so his
exact age no one was really certain about, not even
himself. I discovered later that he didn't even have a
proper birthday, but would celebrate it whenever
he felt like it, just to have an excuse to eat more and
get more presents.) He hadn't reached anything like
the size he was eventually to reach but he was
already podgy, especially about the face. His clothes
– presumably his best ones, though you wouldn't
have thought it to look at them – were tight and
grubby and gave off a funny kind of sheepy smell
whenever he moved. Luckily he didn't move very
often. This last shortcoming was not his fault of
course, but he had also at one time of his life had a
bad go of what is known as the 'cheese sickness' –
the one that the Wanderers bring and that makes
holes all over your skin – and it had left him bald
and mottled and without much in the way of
eyebrows. More like a mucky egg, really, than a
cheese.

None of this would have mattered, at least I don't think it would, not much anyway, had he had other qualities to make up for it. Kindness, for example, or intelligence, or a sense of fun, or else plain humility. Pigs can be fat and ugly and smelly, and yet sometimes they can melt your heart, they are such good company. So can bears. You could tell at a glance, however (*I* could tell at a glance: my parents evidently couldn't or wouldn't), that besides being old and ugly on the outside he was old and ugly on the inside as well: mean, foolish, boring and conceited, and in all likelihood lazy and cowardly as well.

Six serious invisible faults, seven if you add the smell – this sounds just like the unfairness I have promised myself to avoid. I was only twelve, had never met the man before, didn't know very many men anyway, not of this age, not of this kind – how could I tell all these things about him at a glance? I don't know, but I just did. I think it must have been his bad behaviour. One, he didn't bother to move from his chair when I came into the room. Two, he barely looked at me either. Three, the first thing he did after he *had* looked at me was to turn to my father and say, 'Skinny. You'll have to add a couple of more sheep before I sign. Either that, or another bolt of linen.' And four, when my father in reply gave one of his famous snorts and snapped shut the ledger lying open on his knees, he immediately changed his tune and let out a snigger and said he'd only been joking and that the terms they had agreed on suited him fine. They were bargaining, you see, that much I did understand, and it takes nerve to bargain, and this Duke of Wherever-it-was evidently didn't have any or he wouldn't have climbed down so quickly.

All this, as I said, I grasped in a flash, but I can't claim to have been very bright in other ways because the most important thing about the scene, namely, that they were bargaining over *me*, took much longer to sink in.

My father called for Lois and had him bring my flute. 'Play something for the Duke, Alexa,' he ordered. 'Play that birdy thing I like so much, with all the trills.' There was nothing strange in this: I had played for visitors before, and the bird tune was the only one I could get through without making mistakes.

'*Very* nice,' my father said loudly when I had finished, staring hard at the Duke, who looked away and said nothing at all. 'Now do a little dance for us, precious, would you. Pick up your skirts properly so we can see your feet.' This *was* slightly odd, because only Salvans show their feet when they dance, Fanes are supposed to glide. But still, I did as I was told.

After my dance was done my mother retrieved her cushion from the floor where the Duke had dropped it. 'Alexa's work,' she lied, stroking it fondly and brushing off some of the dirt. 'She is so clever with her needle, almost as clever as she is with her pen.'

Do this, do that, turn around, open your mouth, unpin your plaits, add four and five with your hands clasped. But it wasn't really until the Duke, who had watched all these antics in silence without moving at all, save for raising a mottled eyelid now and then, suddenly sat bolt upright in his chair and asked, 'What about eating, though? Eh? Sometimes it's the skinniest ones that need the most feeding' – it wasn't until then that the truth of the matter struck me. Namely, that I wasn't being shown off to a chance visitor, I was being sold.

By my own parents what was more, to this revolting stranger, and without much reluctance from the look and the sound of it. 'Amazingly little,' my mother was quick to reply to the Duke's rude query. 'She eats quite amazingly little for a growing girl. Ask her nurse. Just nibbles at her food. Like a weeny, weeny mouse.'

'Nurse?' The Duke was becoming every moment more attentive. 'You didn't mention the nurse. I thought you said only the soldiers and the two Salvans. I won't have to take on the nurse as well, will I?'

My father opened up the ledger again. 'Wait a moment,' he said. 'Let me just check on that. Retinue . . . number of . . . description of . . . treatment of same . . .'

I listened, still and stiff like the great waterfall and suddenly just as cold. I can't remember if I wanted the answer to this last question to be yes or no, but I rather think I wanted it to be yes, and this shows the depth of my despair. In the normal way of things I would have been only too delighted to be going somewhere Nurse wasn't. So this . . . this lout, this egg-pate, this ancient lump of discourtesy, is to be my future, I thought in horror. This is the man whose wife I am to become, whose house I am to live in and keep in order for him, whose face I am to see every morning on the pillow beside me when I wake and every evening when I go to bed. Agggh! No! Let it not be true! I had always known that I would have to marry young, to someone of my parents' choice, and produce an heir while my father was still alive: it had been dinned into me since the cradle. But I had never thought that it would happen like this, to someone like this.

In panic I tried to catch my father's eye, and then my mother's, but their attention was elsewhere: my father's on his problematic handwriting, my mother's on her rings. It was then, I think, that I knew there was no escape.

'You're right, you know, there's nothing down in black on white,' my father said in a tone of mild surprise, turning the ledger this way and that and shaking it as if to make sure the words hadn't got lost in the binding. 'But I think the Nurse should accompany her all the same, at least for the first fortnight, until she settles down. She has only just turned fourteen, you understand . . .'

'Twel . . .' I started to correct him, but my mother covered up the word with a cough. So that was why the Duke found me skinny: in their eagerness to clinch the match my parents were passing me off as two years older.

'She has only just turned . . . um . . . fourteen, and has led a very sheltered life up to now. I think it would be a comfort for her to have her Nurse with her. Especially since I see here that you have drawn the line at the ponies.'

What was this? No ponies! I was not being allowed to take my ponies! I think I must have cried out at this point, or done something else to make my misery apparent, because my father took one look at me and put aside the ledger and drew me onto his knee in its place, and my mother came over and stood behind us and began pinning up my plaits again with a very light touch, quite unlike Nurse's, and even the Duke moved slightly in his chair and looked vaguely concerned (although I bet it was still Nurse's appetite he was concerned about).

'Let me explain, Your Highness,' he said. It was the first time he had spoken to me directly and I have to admit there was a certain note of kindness in his voice. (But then, so there ought to have been: I mean, if you can't be kind to your future wife on your wedding day, then when can you be?) 'It's not that I forbid the ponies, it's just that the ground around the Castle is too rocky. They would stumble; if you were riding on one you might be hurt. We keep no dogs either, for the same reason.'

He must have seen that the explanation did little to cheer me up because he went on to add, 'We have a lot of birds, though. If you are lonely you could keep some of those.' Keep? Birds fly all over the place, how could you keep a bird? And what sort of place was this, anyway, to which I was going, where not even a dog could hold its footing?

In my bewilderment I tried once more to look into my father's eyes, but he put his cheek close to mine, so that although I felt him near I couldn't really make contact with him, not to ask, not to plead, not to reproach. I was reminded for an instant of the poor Pack Salvans, the ones who carry the wood across the mountain passes on their backs for a living, and of the way they make that sign on their foreheads when they receive their burdens from the loader and murmur, 'So be it, it is the King's will'. Now I knew exactly how they felt.

CHAPTER THREE

My Wedding

ot that I had ever seen one, my parents'
being the last to take place in our
kingdom of Fànes and me being still
in the Sun-god's knapsack at that time, but I had
always imagined royal weddings to be special
occasions: music, banquets, dancing, lengthy preparations beforehand with everybody planning
what to wear and what to eat and where to stand
to get the best view. Even the Miners, according to
Nurse, when a chief's son or daughter got married,
downed tools for the day and left their fires
untended and dressed up in their best and tried
to enjoy themselves. (They didn't dance, of course,
but that was only on account of their feet.)

My own wedding to speckled Duke Raymond
of Crow Mount was a very hurried and shabby

affair, celebrated by the Shaman in his ordinary old fortnight-day cassock, attended only by a handful of people – mostly old women and children, who were the only ones around at that busy moment of the day – and enjoyed, so far as I could see, by no one at all.

We were betrothed in the Thinking Chamber, in the presence of my father's chief counsellor and the Duke's secretary who had accompanied him, only minutes after the meeting I have just described, and were married later that same morning. At sun-zenith as the custom requires; only, as I said, there wasn't any sun that morning, nothing but clouds and rain, so the Shaman had to calculate the right moment by bits of string and guess-work.

How I passed the time between the two ceremonies, I don't remember. Not that it really matters much anyway. I don't think I did any of the packing because Nurse and Sonia took care of that, I don't think I left the castle either, on account of being so tight and uncomfortable inside my dress, and I know I didn't visit the stables to say goodbye to the grooms and the ponies because I just couldn't bear to. Perhaps I took out my knucklebones for a last private game (married women do not play with toys), perhaps I sought the warm, silent company of the Salvans in the kitchen, perhaps I simply slept.

I remember what happened just before the wedding though, and luckily always did remember, even though I was so confused by then that I had difficulty taking things in and might easily have forgotten. As we were all standing around in the banqueting hall, waiting for the smith to deliver the rings which nobody had thought to order until the very last minute, my father put his arm round my shoulders and, still with that cunning technique of holding me close so as not to have to look at me, led me aside into the little corner alcove my mother used to keep her jewels and needles in. 'Business, my little bride-to-be,' he said. 'Affairs of state.'

Once inside he pulled the curtain shut behind us, and after waiting a moment with his eye to a rent in the curtain to make sure no one was outside listening, whispered in a low, urgent voice that he had a great secret to tell me before I left. A secret so important, so vital for all us Fanes, that I was to tell it to no one, save (as he was doing now with me) to the next heir to the throne at the time of his or her marriage.

'Unless you die before that, of course,' he added, sucking at his side-plaits the way he did when something puzzled him. 'In which case you must pass it on *before* your heir's marriage, that's right, before your heir's marriage. And before your own death, otherwise it will be too late. Ha! But not too soon before your own death, because otherwise it will be too soon.' Had he managed to convey the idea, he wondered? And could he trust me with such a secret? Was I old enough to keep it?

'I am fourteen, aren't I, Father?' I could not resist replying, although I knew it was risky to give that sort of answer to a parent and a king. 'If I'm old enough to marry and go and live on the top of a crag with a total stranger, I'm old enough for almost anything don't you think?'

My father loosened his grip on me at this point and turned me round to face him, and asked me with surprising meekness, almost as if I were the parent now and he were the child, not to be angry with him. The marriage was not ideal by any means, he knew that as well as I did, but it was the best offer we were likely to get and we had no choice but to accept it, given the situation. We needed iron and Crow Mount *had* iron. Heaps of it, stacks of it, lying just a palm's width beneath the surface in places. Duke Raymond didn't know this yet because his metal scouts were not as clever as ours, but we did, and we must clinch the deal with him as quickly as possible, before he woke up and realized what he was sitting on. Crow Mount was only half a morning distant on horseback (But I won't *have* a horse! I felt like reminding him, only I knew he would pretend he hadn't heard) and we would see each other often enough. One visit a year had been written into the contract, to take place in the late spring when the avalanches had melted, and if I was a good and sensible wife Duke Raymond would probably allow me more. Especially when I had children: I could

say I wanted to take them to see their grandparents, and the thing would be as good as settled. I
was a Crown Princess, I must remember, not just
an ordinary princess but a Crown Princess, and the
husbands of Crown Princesses tended to be that
much more respectful than other men of their
wives' wishes.

'Is that the great secret then?' I asked. 'About the
iron, I mean?'

'That is *a* secret,' my father said. 'And you
mustn't go telling it to anyone either, particularly
not the Duke, who would think we'd pulled a fast
one on him over the marriage contract. But it is
not the Great Secret. The Great Secret is this' (and
he looked through the peephole again): 'our family
has a pact of alliance with another chieftain's
family, by which we, the Rulers of All the
Fanes, if ever twins are born to us, give the
second-born twin to them to bring up as their
own, and they, in the same situation, do likewise
and give us theirs. We swap twins, so to speak. By
stealth, by night, without anybody but ourselves
knowing what we are up to, we swap our extra
babies. For good and all; no cheating and no trying
to get in touch with the swapped child afterwards.
Once it's gone it's gone.'

'Oh,' I said, and then 'Oh,' again. I did not
know what else to say. If he had told me my
grandmother had been a red squirrel I could hardly
have been more surprised. I didn't think I would

much mind handing over one of my babies to someone else – I didn't want babies anyway, especially not from the Duke – but all the same it sounded an odd, not to say difficult thing to do. Nor, come to think of it, did I greatly relish the idea of suddenly, without warning, having some strange person's baby foisted on me. It struck me, not for the first time that day, that it wasn't as nice as I had thought, being a princess.

My father must have noticed my dismay and put it down to maternal feelings which I didn't have. He stroked my head very gently for him and told me not to worry. Twins were rare, he said, and only large women had them as a rule. Small women, like small dogs, usually dropped only the one. I would never have to abide by the pact myself, he was pretty sure of that, but I had to know about it all the same in order to pass it on to my children and they to theirs and so on, so that the secret would not be lost. And I needn't bother much, either, about taking in a twin from the other family and explaining its presence to the Duke (which to tell the truth might be a little awkward), because apart from the fact that most of their babies died soon after birth anyway on account of the cold, my mother would see to that side of things while she was still alive, that was her affair. She wouldn't like it, mind you, but nevertheless she would grumble and do it.

At the mention of my mother, I wondered for

an instant, aloud, why she wasn't telling me all this herself: surely the smuggling of newborn infants was more a woman's concern than a man's?

My father said a firm no to this, however, and shook his head until his plaits swung. 'The less the matter is mentioned in your mother's hearing the better,' he added. 'It embarrasses her. She's ashamed of our allies, you see. Thinks the whole business of the pact very old fashioned and silly. Says what's the point of an alliance with a tribe that has nothing to offer us but stringy arms and stringy cabbage? Now, I'm not saying she isn't right about this – to be quite honest I can't see much point in it myself – but I know there must *be* a point of some kind, or the secret wouldn't have come down to us the way it has. My great-grandparents wouldn't have told it to my grandparents, I mean, and they wouldn't have told it to my parents, and my parents wouldn't have told it to me, and I wouldn't have told it to you. So there, now you know the arrangement and you must stick by it.'

'But you haven't told me,' I said.

My father's tongue reached out to hook a plait on the upswing. 'Yes I have. This very moment.'

'No you haven't. Not the most important thing. You haven't told me who our allies are, who the family is who gets my extra baby if I have one.'

My father laughed and said my mother was right when she called him a duffer. 'No more I have,' he said. 'Lucky you spotted that one, shows all that copper I spent on your education wasn't wasted. Our ally, little Miss Sharp-wits, is none other than your page Lois's kinsman, the Chief of the Salvans. It is to him and his wife that any second twin of yours, if ever there should be one, is to be delivered.'

Still laughing he closed my mouth for me, which by now was hanging wide open. 'No buts,' he said. 'No squeals like your mother – Uggh! Salvans! Those cave-dwellers! Those marmots! That's the way it is, I am afraid. And don't ask me any more questions, like how and where and when the delivery is made, because one, I don't know the answers, and two, unless I'm very much mistaken you won't be needing them. Now, enough of politics; let's go and find out about those pesky rings.'

The rings had arrived, of course. I had been praying that they wouldn't – anything to hold things up: you never knew, the world might tilt the way the Shaman was always saying it would, and we might all slip off, and no Duke and no marriage and no nothing – but they had. So the wedding took place on schedule, and the Shaman pranced around in front of the menhir with his bells and whatnots and put wet leaves over our heads, and my mother stood there tapping her foot and looking at her dress which was getting spoilt by the rain, and my father gave way to sentiment and blew his nose on his hair. And afterwards we all sat down to a skimpy meal of honey-cakes and undercooked chicken, and the Duke sat next to me at the head of table and ate the best bits of meat and drank a lot of my father's wine, which came from a long way off and was famous for its taste, and made polite but stiff remarks to me, like, 'Very fine salt you have here.' 'Have another walnut.' 'Do you mind the cold?' And then everybody got up and drank our health and sang coarse wedding-songs about rams and vegetables and things, which made me anxious, even though I knew exactly what happened to brides on their wedding nights from spending so much time with the stablemen and listening to their chatter.

And then, with the light already fading over the wreckage of the table and the singing dwindled to the chant of a few single voices (most of them drunken), everyone started wiping their daggers and stuffing them back into their belts and it was time to leave.

I said goodbye to my parents and everybody else present above table-level – I was cross enough to be dignified about it and not to cry – and climbed onto the wagon where Nurse and Sonia were already sitting amidst a heap of trunks and bundles. And once the gate of the castle had been closed behind us I chose the softest of the bundles and curled up on it at Nurse's feet, and shut my eyes and ears and mind, and tried to pretend that I was back at the beginning of the day again, in my own bed, and that none of the events in between then and now had taken place. It was not a courageous thing to do, I know: I should have sat up straight, tried to look cheerful, put on a brave face for Silvia's benefit and for poor down-cast Lois as he loped along rain-sodden beside the wagon. But it was the only thing I was capable of doing.

Nurse must have understood this and had pity on me, because instead of chiding me and telling me I would mess my hair and crumple my dress and look a fright when we arrived at our destina-tion, she let me lie, rocking me a little now and then with the tip of her foot and humming snatches of a lullaby she used to sing when I was a tiny child. At the time I appreciated her switch to tenderness, or thought I did, but looking back on it I'm not sure that it wasn't the worst moment of the entire day: when I realized, that is, that this woman, normally so crabby, so impatient in my regard, actually felt sorry for me in my new life.

CHAPTER FOUR

My Honeymoon

n my first morning as Duchess of Crow Mount (because I was a Duchess now, as well as a Crown Princess. Wouldn't that have been a nice mouthful for Zeno?), I did a wrong and headstrong, and many people would say unforgivable, thing.

Not to excuse myself when there were no excuses, but before I say what thing, I should like first to explain my state of mind on that particular morning. My chats with the stable-men, you must understand, had taught me to look on coupling between the male and female of any species of living being, from beetles to kings, as a natural enough pastime, possibly pleasant, possibly even fun. One look at Duke Raymond and I had ruled out the fun side as far as my own

41

marriage was concerned, but I still expected somehow, even when Nurse was undressing me and
preparing me for his scruffy bed and his scruffy
attentions, that things would take a natural course.
Meaning that they would be all right, acceptable,
bearable. I did not foresee either pain or shame, I
especially did not foresee cruelty.

And yet that is what my husband was to me on
this and the other few nights he lay with me: a
cruel, clumsy, contemptuous lover (lover? well,
hardly, but I know no other word for it), who took
me from the back so as not to see my face, drove
into me with the delicacy, if not the precision, of a
boar-sticker, and left me feeling bruised and used
and dirty, as if I were a dishcloth or a bowl for him
to spit in.

'Do you bleed, Madam?' were the first and
almost only words he uttered on clambering
under the covers beside me. And once I had
understood what he meant and replied that, yes,
as it happened I had started my women's courses
only a few fortnights before, he just grunted and
said, 'Good,' with the air of someone who is
relieved not to be wasting his time. This was all
the courtship he seemed to find necessary. Afterwards, when he had done, he rolled away from me
and said, 'Phew! Paugh! Hope that'll do the trick.'
Which again seemed to suggest effort and reluctance on his part and did not seem to me very
friendly or even very civil. He took to sleeping in a

separate room from then on, but even so the bed smelt of him for fortnights.

When I was older and better at judging people, I discovered more about the man I had married, or been married off to; found out that he did not in fact dislike all women, as Lois always maintained, but only the ones who for some reason posed a threat to him – either because they were weak, or because they were strong, or (which comes to the same thing really when you think about it) because he could not relax in their company. He loved Dolasilla, for example, before the break came; loved her almost more than was good for him, and certainly more than was good for her. He was very fond of his resident mistress – the fat, good-natured old woman who came to greet us when we arrived and who Nurse was so rude to. He was probably quite fond of his sister Rhoda too, in his way. And he must also have loved, or at any rate been loved by, the woman he shared his bed with in the last winter, because I remember being told that when his remains were cast over the ridge (the way that happens to carrion of his kind), she held on so tight to the plank that in the end someone had to drag her away to prevent her from going too. It's funny, isn't it, the way people can be so different, depending on who they are with?

Anyway, that morning I was not only lonely and unhappy but I was offended and hurt. And possibly, being made the way I am, rebellious as well. I sent Nurse packing with a flea in her ear when she came in to dress me (I couldn't play any more maybe now that I was married, but my word I could issue commands); and when a little later on, prompted no doubt by Nurse, Sonia poked her head through the bed-curtains to see if my humour had improved, I think I actually threw a pillow at her.

Eventually, after several of the Crow Mount ladies had also been in to stare at me and ask me if I needed anything and received snarls for their pains, Lois arrived to accompany me on a tour of my new surroundings, to find me still unwashed and un-dressed, curled in my marriage-bed like a cur in its lair.

He didn't say anything, we were still not on talking terms, but instead of goggling at me with curiosity as the others had done, he seemed to know exactly what I was feeling and what I needed in the way of care. First he undid my plaits for me, which were still knotted in the uncomfortable wedding hairstyle Nurse had fashioned the morn-ing before. Then with his nails, which looked crueller than any comb but were in fact surpris-ingly gentle, he began combing them free for me: swish, swish, swish – even the tangles inside my head seemed to straighten out a little under his touch. When he had got all the knots out he pushed my hair back over my shoulders and tied it there loosely with one of the ribbons, then he held up a corner of the bed-linen for me to spit on, the way Nurse sometimes used to when she couldn't be bothered to fetch water, and set about cleaning my face. From there he passed to my neck and ears, and then my hands, which were still clenched so tight he had to prise them open finger by finger. And finally, with an apologetic little moan, as much as to say, I know there are other parts of you that need attention but that is as far as I can go, he knelt down beside the bed and laid his head on my lap, directly over the sore place between my legs, and let it rest there, on top of the bedcovers.

It was then that I behaved so badly. There was spite, you see, in what I did. It was not only the need for comfort: there was recklessness, scorn, revenge, all sorts of nasty things. I didn't just feel, Hold me close Lois, show me you love me; I felt, Go ahead, little creature, help yourself if that is what you want. Who cares how low I sink, who cares, who cares! Anything to hit back, to get even, to render wrong for wrong. What happened to my modesty I don't know, perhaps the Duke's rough treatment the night before had knocked it out of me, perhaps I'd never had any in the first place, but I kicked back the covers, almost disjointing Lois's nose in the process, peeled off my nightshift, threw myself back on the pillows again and lay there stark naked in front of him, holding out my arms and beckoning with my fingers, for anything as if I was one of those fish-women in the Wanderers' songs. And when I saw him start and draw back and shake his head and turn red with shame and then white with longing, I reached out and took him by his thick Salvan's ears and pulled him down onto my lap again – this time with nothing to come between us but his sense of duty. Which was not nearly strong enough to help him resist, poor Lois, because the Salvans are very fiery with respect to coupling, and indeed their enemies say that the only time to catch them off their guard is during the spring when the mating urge is at its highest.

We didn't say anything to one another afterwards, not directly afterwards, that is. I think my extraordinary behaviour had taken us both by surprise. And then there was the question of secrecy: we had taken a terrible risk, if anyone had parted the bed-curtains, as they easily might have done, and found us clinging to one another – Princess and Bodyguard – it would have meant instant death for both of us. He just scrambled off the bed and put his fur to rights, and went to call Nurse to tell her I was ready now for my morning toilet, and then waited outside the bedroom, the way he always did, until I joined him.

Later, however, after he had accompanied me on my round of new household duties (I was beginning to understand my mother's languor now: goodness, the running of a castle looked a dull business, and I hadn't even started yet), I went outside onto the ramparts to get away from the crowd of staring servants and courtiers and hangers-on who had been trailing along behind me all morning, watching my every move, and sat down on a pile of sling-stones, exhausted. And here, with no embarrassment, no hesitation, almost as if it was something we had done all our lives, we at last began to talk, my Salvan shadow and I.

It was I who started the conversation. 'You should have said no, back there in the bedroom,' I said, teasing him slightly, but not exactly mocking, because he looked so forlorn and contrite, crouching there beside the stones. 'You've said it often enough before, so why not this morning? And what about the begging my pardon bit? I don't think I heard that either.'

'This morning was a day apart,' Lois replied, not without a certain dignity. I was surprised at the correctness with which he spoke our Fanish language, but then he'd sat through a lot of Zeno's lessons so I suppose he'd picked it up that way. 'I won't say I'm sorry because I'm not. I love you, you see, Alexa. I always have, I think I always will. But it won't happen again, I promise.'

'I don't mind if it does,' I said. And it was true, I didn't, either one way or the other. 'It is the Duke I mind, it is my horrible, horrible husband. Oh, Lois! Why did they do it? Why did they trade me off like that? Not even my father's horses were ever treated so badly, not even his dogs.'

'How about his Salvans, though?' Lois asked, taking a stone and flinging it with great precision at the flag-staff on a far-off turret.

I saw what he meant, but pointed out that my lot was worse than his and Sonia's. At least they could sleep alone, unmolested. He shrugged and said he wasn't too sure about that. There was no knowing what the Duke's servants might get up to once their initial fright had worn off: they'd never seen Salvans at such close quarters before; might even take it into their heads to chain him and Sonia up at night or something, in case they bit. Not to mention the problem of the winter . . .

I hadn't thought of the winter and didn't want to think of it, so I interrupted him and said quickly, to take his mind off the matter, that for my own part I'd rather be chained up than sleep with the Duke again.

Lois's brow, or what was visible of it, furrowed. 'You'll get used to it,' he said unhelpfully, 'and if you don't you'd better. My mother always used to say, In a difficult fix, sharpen your teeth, in an impossible one, hide them and smile. And this is an impossible fix, Alexa. The Duke is your husband, he can do what he likes as often as he likes. Although . . .' Here he hesitated and crossed his fingers, and then his toes, which I noticed for the first time he was able to do independently, without using his hands. 'Although – I might be wrong about this, so don't build your hopes on it – but I have a sort of feeling he won't bother you very often. Not in that way.'

And then, looking a little embarrassed (which was silly when you think what we'd done together earlier on, but Salvans often are like this I have found: more awkward with words than with actions), he told me his theory about the Duke's dislike of women, and about other things like fatness and laziness and short breath and the after-effects of the cheese sickness, which it seemed disinclined a man in this particular respect. (And please the Sun God it be true, thought I. Please the Sun God and the Deer God and the Moon Maiden and the whole holy lot of them it be true.)

'So, little one,' he wound up, taking my white hand and covering it with his two brown ones so that it looked like the kernel of an outsize nut, 'if you are quick to give him what he wants from you – what they all want from you, which you know as well as I do is an heir to inherit the Kingdom – you may find he will leave you alone altogether.'

The idea of pregnancy revolted me even more than when my father had mentioned it. 'But I don't want the Duke's son!' I almost screamed. 'I don't want any child of his at all!'

'Ah,' said Lois, staring out over the ramparts at the far-off ridge of our own beloved mountains, veiled in mist and hard to recognize, back to front as they were. 'But it may not be his child now. Have you thought of that?'

I hadn't, and when I did it didn't much comfort me, because I couldn't admit this to Lois but the idea of having a Salvan baby was just as bad, if not worse, than that of having a mottled, egg-headed one. Close to despair, I let my gaze follow his: the horizon seemed the only friendly thing in the world at that moment. 'Show me which is Putia, Lois,' I begged of him. 'Talk no more of this heir business. Show me Peres, Sas dla Porta, Col Bechei. And then shut your muzzle.'

'Please.' The relationship between princess and servant had shifted, it seemed, since our traffic on the bed. But he was right to remind me of my manners.

'Please.'

CHAPTER FIVE

The Baby

suppose I must have followed Lois's depressing advice and got used to things, because as the fortnights went by my homesickness for Fànes and my rides and my games and my ponies and everyone and everything I had left behind there did indeed begin to wear off a little. I could still feel it, but it was an ache now rather than a pain, and you can live with an ache, you can live quite well.

Not everything about my new life was hateful. In fact some things were really rather nice. No more lessons, for example. Nobody (not even Lois who was a companion now, not just a bodyguard) to tell me what not to do. And no more of Nurse's huffs and moods and hair-brushings: she left as arranged, a fortnight after our arrival, half-starved according to her, but full of exciting news to tell my mother, about how bad the food was at Crow Mount, and how coarse the linen, and how lazy the servants, and how altogether inferior the whole set-up was to the one she was used to. She was another piece of home lost to us, but neither Sonia nor Lois nor I was particularly sorry to see her go.

Then there were the birds. Duke Raymond had spoken the truth: Crow Mount had birds by the thousand, the way other places have fleas or mice. (Only being birds, of course, they were more beautiful and better behaved.) In the early morning, when the slops were thrown out over the rocks, you could hear them whirling in for the feast in such numbers that the flapping of their wings stirred the air like a wind; and if you looked out of the window, as I always did if I was awake and it was not too cold to leave the bed, you would see a great dark mass like a storm-cloud, hovering over the battlements and then swooping down into the ravine with a mastery my brother would have envied. They were mostly crows and starlings, but there were jackdaws among them too, and sparrows and blackbirds and robins and many others whose names I didn't know. And here and there, disdainful of the slops and the jostling but not wanting to miss the party, you would see, circling above the cloud on the lookout for a different kind of breakfast, hawks, kites, and even the occasional eagle.

The Baby

I got to look forward to this moment of the day, and from the supper table would bring up leftovers in my châtelaine's stomach pouch, to spread on the windowsill and lure the birds closer. I did it quite openly too: now Nurse was gone, who dared tell a Crown Princess/Duchess that such a thing was messy or wasteful?

I also, funnily enough, got quite interested in my daily household duties – for a while anyway, until they became routine. You would think, as I did myself at the start, that supervising the clothing and feeding of the hundred and more people who lived and worked inside the castle of Crow Mount would be about as much fun as sorting pepper-corns, perhaps less. But it was not so. For one thing, people are more varied than peppercorns: there are nice ones, nasty ones, shy ones, brash ones, honest ones, dishonest ones, all sorts and all mixtures, and it is a far subtler game than chequers to try to work out who is which. For another thing, counting stores is not just counting stores, slippety-sticks the way my mother did, it is planning, it is politics. If the counts don't tally between cellar and kitchen, or between kitchen and table, it means rustling is going on. I discovered this almost the first day. But I also discovered that rustling is not always what it seems to be, and that there are right forms of rustling (such as Luna's, the kitchen maid's, who it turned out was putting aside the food for her brother: an outcast with the Bone-rot and no one to care for him at all), and wrong forms of rustling that nonetheless must be allowed because to interrupt them would be indelicate. (I am thinking here of old Hubert and his 'clients'. What harm was there, I mean, in his hiding away the odd bale of hay and selling it to the Wanderers the way he did? He didn't do it for the gain, it was just that it gave him a sense of his lost importance.)

The linen check, too, had a pleasant side to it: there is something sane, something soothing, I have always found, in piles of well-washed, well-tended linen. In fact it has such a calming effect on me that later on, in what the singers used to call the Glorious Years but I now think of as the Years of Rabies, I can remember on more than one occasion leaving the rest of the household to its bashings and clankings, and climbing up to the turret where the linen chests were kept, and opening them and laying my cheek against the clean lavender-scented contents in search of – yes, sanity, that is the only word for it: a tiny store of sanity in a world gone mad.

Lois's guess was correct, thank goodness, and the Duke paid me scarcely any more nightly visits. He paid me very little attention in the daytime also, so that apart from our places at table, him at one end, me at the other, you would hardly have known we were man and wife. This in turn – his lack of attention, I mean, his lack of regard – seemed to make me better liked by the other people in the castle, especially the serving people, and I began to make a few new friends: Tilly the head store-keeper, Baldur the falcon-feeder, and a strange old man who seemed to have no particular job and no particular skill but who everybody went to for advice all the same, called Mulebones on account of his thinness, or Muley for short.

So one way and another, after what had felt like an impossible beginning, I was managing to cope with my new life, finding a way of coming to terms with it.

But, as Lois says his mother used to say in yet another of her cheerful and original proverbs, Nothing is sure in this world except that nothing is sure. No sooner had I found my feet, or begun to, than they were knocked away from under me: I discovered I was pregnant. Me, the choosy, the wilful, the lone rider, the fastidious dresser – I was expecting a baby. By the toad or by the marmot, it made little difference: an unwanted being was growing inside me, stretching my clothes so that they didn't fit me any more, stretching my stomach so that I could no longer sleep in the position I liked, hampering my movements, weighing me down like a burden. Once again I was reminded of the wretched Pack Salvans and their, 'It is the King's will'. It was the King's will, and the Queen's my mother's, and the Duke's my husband's, it was everybody's will but mine.

The winter had set in when I was sure of what was happening, when I could no longer deny it even to myself. This made it even more difficult to bear. I would have liked to have confided in Sonia – we had grown very close to one another now, little red-pawed Sonia and I – but she had gone into her torpor fortnights back and was now lying safely in the bottom of one of my clothes chests, out of sight from prying eyes, curled up like a dormouse and with nothing to say for herself but 'Mmmm' and 'Zzzz' and 'Leeeave me beeee'. So there was not much comfort to be had from her.

Lois on the other hand was still awake, or sort of, fighting against sleep with a doggedness that touched my heart. He said he would kill himself rather than leave me unguarded until springtime, and I think he meant it. At nights he lay outside my bedroom door in a sack made of sheepskin – he claimed the heat kept him more wakeful than the cold, which was funny because it's the other way round with me – and in the daytime he kept himself going by drinking nettle juice and stand-ing on his head whenever the urge to nod off became too strong. He looked a fright – all eyes and bones – and even the Duke noticed and suggested at one point we should stow him away in the cellars somewhere and send for Tecla instead as was laid down in the contract, but Lois wouldn't hear of it and kept to his watch.

I could have turned to Lois for comfort, then,

instead of sleepy Sonia, but for some reason I didn't want to. I suppose I understood even then that it would not be tactful to let him know the way I really felt about the baby. So finally, before announcing the bad/good news to the Duke and everyone and enduring all the fuss I knew it would lead to – bonfires on the towers, kisses from the ladies, proddings in the stomach from the Crow Mount Shaman and goodness knows what else – I went to look for Muley and told him.

I haven't really described Muley yet, but then he is very hard to describe because there was nothing particularly noticeable about him. Until you got to know him well, that is, when you would begin to realize that he was special, although you still couldn't say why or in what way. He was sort of smallish and greyish, and very quiet of voice and movement. His eyes were blue, or had been once; now they were the colour of evening snow. He was very clean for an old man and very precise with his words. If he said something, it was because he had grounds for it. Most people you speak to come out with things like, Wanderers are horse-thieves, Redheads bring bad luck, just because they have heard them and are repeating them; I do it myself when I'm not careful. But Muley was different, he thought things over. If he ever gave you advice, therefore, which he seldom did because he pre-ferred listening to talking, it was worth following. I hadn't been in Crow Mount six full moons yet and was still on my guard with almost everybody, but him I trusted like a lifelong friend. Mainly, I suppose now, because that was his speciality – getting people to trust him.

That morning, when I told him about my plight, he was so sweet and understanding I could have hugged him. He put his hands gently on the place the baby was to feel if it was moving, and told me not to worry, not to fret, even asked me if I wanted to be rid of it, which was something I didn't even know was possible.

We were sitting under the stairs, I remember, in the closet he used in those days as his bedroom and living room and workplace and everything. 'Possible?' he echoed with a chuckle. 'Ah, Your Highness! Your dear little ignorant Highness! Of course it is possible. Just leave it to Muley, everything is possible with Muley. Place yourself in his hands and, snicker snack, we'll send the bundle back to the Sun God again.'

I wonder what would have happened if I had said yes. I very nearly did, only for some reason the word 'bundle' conjured up in my mind the image of the real baby lying inside me all crinkly and curled up and defenceless like Sonia in her chest, and the 'snicker snack' made me think of harm coming to it through no fault of its own, and I said no instead. Quite a loud no, almost a shout.

'Then no be it, Highness,' Muley approved. He was always very quick to understand other people's feelings. 'No sending back. We will keep it and we will love it.'

This sounded reassuring but very unlikely. 'Will we? Will I? *Love* it? Are you sure?'

Muley paused to think the way he always did, then crinkled his eyes at me and nodded. 'From the first moment it breathes,' he said, 'and do you know why? Because it will be beautiful like yourself, and brave like yourself, and good tempered like yourself, and once it is born you will stop feeling lonely and wonder what you ever did without it.'

Already I felt better: it is hard to disagree with someone who tells you you are brave and beautiful and good tempered. 'It won't take after Duke then?'

Muley shook his head. 'Not the Duke as he is now,' he said. 'He wasn't always like that, you know; when he was young he was quite passable to look at. Have no fear, Highness, you will have a nice, ordinary, healthy baby with clear skin and plenty of hair and eyebrows, I promise.' Then he put his hands back on my stomach again and frowned slightly. 'A bit on the big side, mind you, but otherwise, no, a perfectly nice baby in every way.'

CHAPTER SIX

The Babies

After this conversation with Muley I settled down a little and, as over the business of the marriage, tried to make the best of things. Duke Raymond was so excited at the news of the baby he almost rose from his chair to congratulate me, and on his special orders I was given bigger helpings at mealtimes and lighter duties. At table on the next feast day he made me the present of a copper circlet to wear in my hair, but in private took it away again, saying that I would get it back after the birth. It would be a waste, he explained, to have to bury it in the ground with my ashes if I died in labour, the way so many women seemed to do. Better to wait until after. I'm not sure I wouldn't have preferred no circlet and no explanation, but anyway, it was a gesture.

And to do him justice the Duke was right to be cautious about his gift: I very nearly did die in labour. I remember little about the whole business myself, only the pain and the confusion and the shouting of the midwife when I grabbed her, and the Shaman's voice coming through the curtains, yelling instructions which no one seemed to follow, least of all myself. 'Push!' Push what for goodness' sake? Push how, when they were pinning me down like a rabbit skin? 'Stop fighting against the pain! Go with it!' Not on your life, Master Shaman, *you* go with it if you're so keen. 'Relax, it is over now. All over. All over. The baby is born.' Born? You liar. Nothing is over yet, nothing is finished except me.

Eventually I must have fainted, and this was a good thing for several reasons. One because the midwife was able to do what she had wanted to do from the beginning only I hadn't let her, and that was to hook her finger under the stuck baby's armpit and yank it out by force (like all good midwives she was a very forceful woman under all the twittering). Two because I didn't have to be there, not the feeling part of me anyway, while this was going on. And three because after I had fainted everyone thought that I was dead, and covered me up with a sheet and paid no attention to me, and consequently didn't see my face when I learnt the awful truth, namely that I had given birth not to one baby but to two – to twins, twin daughters, with all that that entailed from the point of view of the Great Secret.

So much for my father's predictions about small women, and so much for my own careless attitude about respecting the pact and giving one of my newborn creatures away. I can't say I took to Dolasilla and Lujanta from their first breaths the way Muley said I would – I was too tired, too weak to take much notice of either. Nor did I feel anything resembling love for them: they were far too slippery and dirty and strange, and I was glad to see them taken charge of by others and carted off to the nursery so that I could get some sleep. But from the moment the midwife brought them to me the next morning, all clean and cuddly and wrapped up in their bands like a pair of little white grubs, and laid them on the bed and said, 'There, now, aren't they just the wolfcub's whiskers!' I felt a bond with them so strong that, although they were separate people now, they might still have been part of my body.

I was reminded of my father's hunting bitch Lea, and of how difficult it had been to get her to leave her puppies, even for walks. I had been cross with her at the time and had dragged her out with me willy nilly, but now I could understand: she had felt linked to those creatures of hers, that was it, linked, needed, responsible, and wherever she went she had felt the pull. From then on, as I sat there looking down at Dolasilla's round pink face and Lujanta's pointed orange one, and at Dola's droopy eyelids and Lulu's slanting ones, and at Dola's stubby fingers and Lulu's funny little mole-claws, I began to feel it myself.

And the pact? Well, I tried not to think about it. Muley said a baby would cure my loneliness, and he was talking about one: two babies made me forget loneliness had ever existed. It was a good time, of course, in other ways as well. The Duke not only gave me the circlet, he gave me a pet owl and a new dress and a donkey to make up for the ponies, and took to calling me Alexa instead of Madam. His sister, the pillow-chested Rhoda, stopped treating me as if I were a piece of sift-cloth she could see right through, and spoke to me once or twice quite agreeably, even offered to tell the babies' fortunes for me, which was something she was supposed to do well, being barren and a squinter. (I couldn't allow it, of course, just in case she really did have the gift.) Everybody in fact was kinder to me than they had been on my arrival, made allowances for me, smiled instead of staring and waiting for a slip-up.

Spring was on the way, Lois was perking up, Sonia was stirring, I could fit into my dresses, even if they were getting rather short at the hemline – life was becoming almost fun again. It was still peace time too in the region, and whereas peace time in Fànes had simply meant that there were no real battles with the neighbouring tribes, only raids and beatings-off and skirmishes too small to count, at Crow Mount peace was truly peace. I think we had our position to thank for this more than the Duke's politics: not even the foxes seemed to want to make the long climb up to raid the chicken coops, not even the wolves seemed to think prowling at that altitude worth their while. The only smoke we saw that winter, apart from our own fires, was from the charcoal burners' camps in the woods below, the only clank of metal we heard was from the chains of the drawbridge when it was pulled up for the night and let down again in the morning. (And sometimes not even that, because the gatekeeper couldn't always be bothered.)

All went smoothly, therefore, until the day I decided to take the twins out into the castle courtyard for a ride on the donkey. The court-yard, mark you, not the rocks, not the ramparts: just a tame little spin round the courtyard to give them some fresh air and get some spring sun on their faces. It didn't seem at the time a particularly risky thing to do, and nobody, not even the Duke, appeared to think so either: he even had Muley make a special pair of panniers to put across the donkey's withers to carry the babies in, without lids on. (Lucky the idea was his, I dread to think what would have happened if it had been mine.)

There were no upsets the first time round and the donkey behaved beautifully. The people in the courtyard smiled and clapped and called out the twins' names, and said 'May the Sun God bless them!' and 'Look what poppets!' and 'Ooochie, oochie!' and all the silly things people say to babies, and some of the castle children ran on in front and others tagged on behind, until we formed quite a procession.

As we started on our second lap, however, there was a sudden disturbance and a noise like a piece of cloth being torn – Craaah! The children screamed and fell back, the donkey swerved, and I, who had been keeping my eyes on the twins' faces to make sure they were enjoying themselves, saw them pass from bright sunlight into dark shadow in a trice. I looked up, but it was too late by then, and the eagle – because that was what it was that cast the shadow: a great brown she-eagle with wings as big as breadloaves – was already swooping towards Lulu's basket with its talons out, ready for the snatch.

I should, the shepherds told me afterwards, have flapped around with my skirts and arms to create confusion, or else yanked at the donkey's bridle and got it to zig-zag. What I should not have done, and what needless to say I did, was to make a grab for the threatened baby, because this only helped the eagle to concentrate and tighten its grip after it had made its strike.

All very well, but I would have liked to see a shepherd defending, not a lamb, but one of his own children. Who could think of skirt-swishing or donkey-driving at such a moment? There was no time to think of anything. I shrieked (another mistake apparently: you shriek before the attack, not during), lunged out, saw the talons sink into Lulu's wrappings, felt the wrappings tighten in my hands as the eagle rose again, and then snap with a jerk as it broke away, and it was all over: Craaah! Whoosh! Plick! Three lightning stages and then there was nothing to do but watch the bird disappear over the battlements with its little white prize.

Through all the uproar that followed, one of the children kept plucking at my dress and babbling something about a string – the eagle had had a string attached to its leg, he kept saying, its beak had been tied up with string too, he had seen it, he was sure – but I didn't pay any attention to this detail until later. I was too miserable, too shaken, too angry really, to do anything but clutch my one remaining baby in my arms and continue my shrieking.

I ran outside the castle – we all did. I yelled for the archers, I yelled for my own Fane soldiers. 'Do something!' I screamed at them. 'Find the bird! Shoot it! No, don't! Follow it, see where it goes!' But there was nothing to see or find *or* shoot. The eagle had vanished, apparently into thin air (although I now realize it must have been drawn by the string into some hiding place on the ground), and Lulu with it.

That night however, as I lay in my bed, still clutching onto Dola who had hardly been out of my arms since, the child's words came back to me, and I began to feel a tiny flickering of hope. An eagle with its beak bound, an eagle on a string, like a dog on a leash – could this mean it had been a tame eagle? On an errand, so to speak? Could it be something to do with the pact and the Salvans? The Salvans were famous for the way they handled animals, my father used to say they could tickle the bellies of wolves. Could it be, then, that my baby was not dead as I feared, but safe in some high mountain cave with its new adoptive parents?

I hung on to this hope for two days, not allowing it to grow any bigger, but not allowing it to dwindle either. I needed it because they were two difficult days. Duke Raymond didn't seem to mind the loss of Lujanta the way I minded it – he even commented when he was told the news, 'Lucky it was the dark one that went,' which was a thing I never would have said or thought myself, both twins being equally precious to me – but he minded. Perhaps it was a question of pride, dignity, of word getting round that he had been cheated by a bird, I don't know, but anyway he took the loss badly. And having nobody in particular to punish, he punished more or less everybody. He had a grisly kind of fake funeral performed, with a doll on the pyre to represent Lujanta, made out of wax and wool: to this day I feel sick when I smell freshly lighted tapers. He organized a massive bird-shoot, followed by another nasty-smelling bonfire. He had the Shaman cleanse me of traces of the evil eye, and then obliged me to stand by and watch while the same treatment of cold sluicings and garlic-rubbings was meted out to poor little Dolasilla – who caught a fearful cold afterwards as a result so that we nearly lost her too, as well as Lulu. He took Muley's wicker-making tools away and had them smashed and forbade him basket-work for ever. He ordered a whole day's silence and fasting, and made all those who had been in the courtyard at the time of the eagle's swoop crawl in front of him on their hands and knees and beg his pardon for not having seen the bird sooner, even the children. Silliest and cruellest of all to my mind, he had the donkey beaten.

Then, on the third day, when hope was giving out, a little parcel appeared mysteriously in my bedroom, all done up in leaves and heather, and when I opened it I found inside two pieces of string, one short, one very, very long, and Lujanta's swaddling bands, carefully folded. There was no message included but I didn't really need one: however nimble they may be with their talons, eagles do not rewind string or fold clothes or deliver parcels. So from that moment on I knew Lulu was safe – as safe as she could be in the circumstances, for hadn't my father said something dreadfully worrying about the cold? – with the Salvans.

It was not much by way of consolation but it was something. Later that spring, when I went back to Fànes with Dolasilla for my first visit, my parents tried to cheer me up by telling me how well they thought the whole thing had gone off, considering.

'So clever of the Salvans,' my mother said. 'Making it look like an accident the way they did, and nobody to blame but an eagle. I couldn't really think of a better way myself.'

'Nope,' agreed my father. 'Cunning little blighters, cunning as weasels. Got the right baby too, first time off: the second born, just like the pact says. I wonder how they managed that?'

To tell the truth I wondered about that myself and still do. But there are lots of things about the Salvans that I have yet to learn. In their practical way they are a very kind-hearted people, however, and every year, at the exact time of Lulu's disappearance, I would receive the same heather-wrapped parcel containing different things. Sometimes it would be a snippet of hair, sometimes a tooth, sometimes (to show me how big she was, I suppose, and how well cared-for) a stocking or a shoe or a complete dress. With these, and the scant but vital information they gave me, I had to be content.

CHAPTER SEVEN

The Miners

fter the disappearance of Lujanta in the eagle's claws we had several really quiet humdrum years in which nothing more terrible happened than the sacking of the apple harvest by an army of earwigs, and the burning of half the laundry when it was hit by lightning. The soldiers of my guard were recalled to Fànes: there was no point in keeping them just for the occasional onslaught of bugs. I think of it as a good period now, but I was young then and eager for adventure, and while it was happening I found it rather dull. Just shows what difficult creatures we humans are to please.

The seasons passed. It snowed and then the snow melted and the flowers came out. Sonia went in and out of her chest, Lois watched over us, Rhoda grew fatter on the top and the Duke grew fatter all round, Muley's hair turned from grey to white, and I grew taller and taller and then stopped. We all grew older. I went back to Fànes each year, and each year noticed slight but definite changes. Some of them pleasant, like the softening of Nurse's temper (she doted on Dolasilla and would do anything for her, even bend to pick up her toys); some of them sad, like the death of two of my ponies from old age, and the retirement of the head stableman, who went blind overnight one winter, nobody knew why, and was only fit afterwards to sit in the kitchen with the Salvans and peel vegetables.

The changes at Crow Mount I noticed less, because I spent more time there and had more to do. My days were mostly happy, because my days were mostly Dolasilla and Dolasilla was happy. Never before and never since have I seen a more beautiful, healthy, perfect child. Everybody has a flaw of some kind: even if you are born straight-limbed and straight-eyed and straight-toothed, which few of us are, there are the biffs and buffetings along the way that leave their mark – a scar here, a gap there, a break and a bend somewhere else. Even I, who was protected from the cradle like a sacred oak-shoot, have a slightly chipped tooth in the front from a fall when I was little which Lois couldn't cushion. Not to mention the Duke, and what the cheese sickness did to him.

But Dola, no, Dola was faultless. She shone with

health, she bulged with strength and energy. People couldn't look at her without smiling and widening their eyes with respect for such a small being that yet could contrive to be so powerful. 'Filthy misery!' the shepherds and foresters used to exclaim as we passed them on our rambles (it was not a swear-word but their way of saying 'Goodness!' or 'Good heavens!'). 'Filthy misery, what hair, what skin, what colours! Looks like she's made of corn and dough and poppy petals!' I have never held with shifting our mistakes onto Fate, that is the coward's way, but it strikes me now that it was indeed Dola's destiny to conquer; even if she had been born in the smelt-pits of Mill Brook I think she would have won her way out somehow. She had everybody at her feet from the cradle onward: not only the softies like me and Sonia and Lois, but the real toughnuts like the Duke and Nurse and my parents. When I took her to Fànes my mother used to sit her on her knee and go quite broody with grandmotherly love, and look quite hurt, what was more, when Dola, as she nearly always did, squirmed and kicked and wriggled to be free. If characters are susceptible to spoiling, like a sauce or a junket when it curdles, then I reckon this was how and when we spoilt her: early on and from too much love.

When she was old enough to start lessons I began to appreciate what my father had said about Zeno and the pig bristles. We sent out word via the

Wanderers that we were looking for a tutor, and over the following months several candidates turned up at our gates in answer to the summons, but none of them was any good at all. The first, rather like my mother with her numbers, only did pretend writing: it looked very fine on the page, but when you went to read it there were no letters there, only long spindly chains of ink. (The man was very offended when I pointed this out, and said he had taught at the court of the King of Cadubren for years without anyone ever complaining, and I discovered much later on this was perfectly true, he had.) The second may have known a thing or two – he had all sorts of tricks in his bag: a counting frame, a disc with stars on it, a funny jointed stick for measuring corners – but we had no language in common, and he just stood there with his instruments, babbling at me, and I (to his way of thinking, I suppose: in fact I was being very apologetic and polite) just babbled back, and that was that. Nagra, as the Miners say when the rock won't cleave. Nothing doing.

After these we had a couple of professional wise men, of the sort that write out people's names for them at fairs, but they both wrote very slowly with their tongues sticking out and got their fingers messier than my father's. Then came a hunchback, who looked serious and capable to me, but whom the Duke (if you please!) turned down on grounds of ugliness. Then we had a visit from the one-time teacher of the Prince of the Cajutes, who we couldn't accept because he might have been a spy. Then an escaped prisoner on the run with the rings still on him. Then a madman as dark as charcoal. Then a mouth-frother. It went on like this for ages.

Finally, one meal time, after the fifteenth or sixteenth candidate had come and gone and we were no nearer a solution, Duke Raymond gave a great belch and, reverting to 'Madam' as he always did when he was cross, bellowed out for all to hear, 'A plague on all these time-wasters! I will not have our daughter grow up unlettered. Learn her yourself, Madam, if you can find no other!'

Learn her yourself. Well, at least I could do a little better than that. At this point, however, a voice piped up from somewhere in the shadows, 'Let me try, your Grace. Sometimes what you are looking for is so close you cannot see it. Let me have a try at being tutor.' And believe it or not it was Muley. Our own man-of-all-trades-and-none Muley.

We all thought he was joking to begin with, but when he insisted he was in earnest I put him through his paces and found to my surprise that he could read and write and calculate faster than a horse could bolt. When had he learnt and from whom? Nobody knew, and he wouldn't say; just smiled and looked mysterious and murmured his usual, 'Muley can do anything if he puts his mind to it'. But anyway, there he was, right under our noses – the perfect schoolmaster for Dola, and very cheap too because all he wanted in return for his services was a bigger and brighter room in place of his cubby-hole under the staircase.

For the first few months I sat through Muley's lessons myself, to make sure he was doing things right. Then I was busy with the spring cleaning and didn't bother, and by the time I went back to the schoolroom again he and Dola were onto subjects so new to me that I could no longer keep up with them, let alone judge how well they were getting on. They did what were called 'tables', but I only saw one table myself: the one that they worked on. They did 'operations', I don't know what these were either. They dismantled sentences as if words were solid things like stones you could build a house of, and juggled them around to make new ones. They did memory games, and studied things called 'figures' which were words and not figures at all, and other things called 'fallacies', which I seem to remember were bad ways of trying to win an argument (although if you win, any way seems good to me). They all had weird and difficult names, these fallacies, and Muley said they came from another language, far richer and more beautiful than ours, which I doubt because it sounded hideous to me – all 'arums' and 'orums' and 'ibuses'. Very soon Dola was writing, not the same sentence over and over again like I had done with Zeno, but all sorts of different ones, amounting sometimes to whole stories. I was so admiring and so envious that I practised a lot on my own, in my room at night, in an effort to catch up with my baby daughter. (Which I never did, but at least I became a bit niftier with my pen in the process.)

Our lives could (and perhaps should) have gone on like this for ages: rumpity tumpity, strum strum strum, like music played on the zither without the interference of drumbeats or cymbal clashes. My father had other plans, however, and had had them from the start. After waiting for what I suppose he considered this tactful length of time, long enough to seem appreciative but not downright greedy, he at last laid claim to the mining rights he had acquired with my marriage, and began digging into the mountainside round Crow Mount in search of the metal ore he knew was there and the Duke didn't. And with this action, peace as we knew it came to an end.

I say laid claim to the mining rights, but really he just took them. And very fast and firmly too. One evening we went to our beds surrounded by nothing but mist and darkness and sleeping birds, and the next morning, when we woke, it was to find ourselves in what looked like the grip of a besieging army. There were camp-fires dotted around everywhere, and in the light of each fire you could see dozens of strange little people scuttling to and fro, unpacking things and cooking things and putting up shelters and generally settling themselves in for what promised to be a long stay, right there on our very doorstep almost. The birds circled round above them, perplexed, miffed by the disturbance to their nesting grounds.

The Duke, once his fright had worn off, was furious, and in this case I couldn't entirely blame him. 'Rights or no rights, this is no way to go about things, Madam,' he puffed at me indignantly over the entire length of the breakfast table. 'Stealing up on us overnight, and not so much as an if you please or a by your leave. Your father has the manners of a mud-hog! He should have warned us of the arrival of his Miners. I could have given him assistance. Now I'm blowed if I'll give him so much as a log or a drop of water, not even if he comes to beg of me in person.'

I think Duke Raymond probably stuck to this threat as he stuck to most, but if he did nobody gave him the satisfaction of noticing. The Miners were quite extraordinary in the way they were equipped and organized. They brought everything with them, from the huge great pine-trunks with which they timbered their shafts, down to the tiny neat little splinters with which they picked their teeth after meals. In a sense, what with the smoke and the smells and the ventilating machines, I suppose you could say they even brought their own air.

The Miners

I was fascinated to watch them. I had never seen
Miners in the flesh before, although I had heard a
lot of stories about them from Nurse, whose
brother had worked in Mill Brook as a middle-
man and knew them well. I expected monsters, all
bent and scuttling like spiders, with twisted limbs
and sightless eyes and hearts as black as their faces,
but reality is never quite like the stories. They were
maimed, a lot of them, of course – some from falls,
some from being hit by falling materials, some from
the terrible flesh-eating vapours that wear away
fingers and toes without the owner even noticing
until it is too late. Their skins were a funny colour
too, even after washing, and their eyes were weak,
like moles' are said to be, and they coughed and
spat a lot, and had worms and fleas and all sorts of
creepy-crawlies, and the tallest among them hardly
reached my waist, nevertheless they were unmistakably people and not spiders. Very nice people
they seemed too, when you became friends with
them and sat just the right distance away.

With Dola and Muley at my side, who were
even more intrigued by our new visitors than I
was, I followed all the stages of their work. (All the
stages, that is, that we were *allowed* to follow: some
were so secret the Miners wouldn't even talk about
them to outsiders, let alone show them.) How do
you get something precious out of the depths of
the earth which the earth is not willing to part
with? Well, the answer is that you strive for it with

every means at your disposal, but especially with your noddle. First you have to know where to dig and how deep. The scouts had already reported the presence of metal ore in great quantities, but the Miners weren't content with the reports and spent the first fortnight of their work down on all fours like dogs, sniffing out for themselves what they called the 'veins' and the 'drifts' and the 'stringers'. By which they meant the underground pathways that the ore follows. It was as thrilling as a hunt: you would see them scanning the ground for the signs that only they knew how to read – a bare patch, a darkening of the earth, a change of colour in the moss – and then one of them would lift up his or her head and make a funny Oyoyoy! noise and the others would leave their scanning and run to where the shout came from and, fanning themselves out into a line, would begin scuffling in the ground with their tools. If the pathway, or vein, was a good one, if it didn't stop suddenly, or wind in the wrong direction, or break up into smaller pathways, as many of them seemed to do, they would mark it out with little red pegs, call for the Chief (who did something very secret at this point to check the nature of the metal, but I couldn't tell what, because he did it under cover of his cloak), and then sit down all together and celebrate by taking a swig of their famous fire-water. If it was a very good vein they would take several swigs, and if it was a very, *very* good one they would give it a name and drink its health and take so many swigs that the day's work usually ended there, with the naming ceremony.

By the end of the fortnight we had the River Vein (wide), and the Thread Vein (narrow), and the Worm Vein (wiggly), and Jaco's Vein (discovered by a little Miner boy called Jaco), and the Fox Vein (which fooled everyone for a bit by dipping deep underground and coming up somewhere else: the Miners were not very imaginative with their naming), and dozens of smaller unnamed veins with lots of stringers branching off them, and piles of empty flasks, and wuzzy heads galore, and the Chief of the Miners beat his gong to call an end to the search and announced it was time to pass to the next phase and sink the shafts.

Only shafts don't sink, of course, nothing so easy: they have to be driven down into the earth by force of arm-power, and the earth has to be removed, stone by stone and bucketful by bucketful. Nor are they, as I imagined to begin with, before I saw one or went down one, just holes in the ground. No, they are great timbered corridors, big enough for three people to crawl down abreast and three more to crawl up with loads on their backs. There has to be air inside the shafts too, or ways of getting air inside, or the Miners would suffocate; and if there is too much water at the bottom there have to be ways of getting the water out, or the Miners would drown; and if there isn't enough water it has to be brought in because a certain amount is needed for the sluicing of the rock-face. This second phase of the work, therefore, although one of the riskiest, was not so much fun to watch as the others, and Dola and Muley and I spent most of our time squatting round the camp-fires with the Master Diggers (who were not called on to work at this stage, being far too skilled and important), listening to their stories and trying to learn the ins and outs of their extraordinary trade. It was then that I first heard of firing and dousing and splitting, of spiking and blocking and wedging and roasting and assaying, and all those other processes (save one or two they were careful not to mention) that would soon become so familiar to me. It was then, too, I think, when he tried in vain to draw the Miners out on the subject of their gold and how they made it and where they kept it, that I first saw a strange bright-coloured light flicker in the snow of Muley's eyes, but I didn't really pay much attention to it: I thought it must just be the reflection of the flame from the Miners' fire.

Once the shafts were in place the Chief paid another top-secret visit to the galleries to mark out the best places for hewing, and then the excitement started up again. The Master Diggers put on their leather aprons and their waist-high boots and their leather caps with the candle on the front, and disappeared down the mouth of the first shaft, singing one of their special songs to placate the anger of the Earth Goddess. (Who they were very rude about, incidentally, above ground, and called a cussed old B, but now seemed to fear immensely, and with good reason.) They were followed by the carriers, who did not sing at all or even speak, but crept down into the earth in deathly silence: all you could hear was the flapping of their empty skin bags and the squeak of their baskets. (Carrying was such hard work, we were told, they had to save their breath. But, myself, I wouldn't mind betting they'd had orders to keep their mouths shut, in case, in the heat of the excitement, they babbled.)

Soon afterwards, much sooner than I had expected, the carriers were back again, bent double under their loads, and the first pieces of mined ore were hauled out of the earth and into the sunlight. The stuff looked like plain old stones to me, but at the sight of it the rest of the mining people, who up till then had been hopping nervously round the entrance to the shaft, whispering and listening and biting what remained of their fingernails, gave a great howl of triumph: Fer! Fer! Fer! You would think all the ore was theirs from the noise they made, not only the twentieth part which was their due.

Then, fast as ants latching onto a dead bee, they set to work: sorting the newly mined material into piles, chipping it and pounding it with their hammers, washing it in sieves so as to see how rich it was, and then sorting it all over again and placing the best bits on little wheeled carts which ran downhill on wooden runners and tipped out their contents at the bottom, building them into a special heap. Which grew and grew and grew as the morning advanced, until it formed a mountain of its own on the flank of the mountain.

That's what I mean about using your noddle: the Miners were full of devices like these for making their work lighter. They had runnels, winches, giant bellows, buckets on chains, all sorts of wonderful things. I know – even about the underground machines they tried to keep secret – because Muley used to creep down the shafts and study them when nobody was looking and make models of them for Dola to play with. (That at any rate was what he called them when I asked about them: playthings.)

When all the veins had been worked, however, and the mines were empty, and it came to taking the ore back to Fànes for smelting, there were no machines strong enough and no ideas clever enough, and my father had to call in his faithful Pack Salvans to do the work. I remember watching their old foreman, Pepi, as he took his instructions from the Chief of the Miners. The ore had grown almost as big as a real mountain now, and Pepi stood in its shadow, listening, bowing, meekly accepting, as small as a mouse beside a haystack. I wanted to call out to him (I felt much closer to the Salvans now on account of Lulu, almost like a relation): 'Don't do it! For goodness' sake don't do it. You will die, all of you! The weight will break your backs!' But before I could do so I saw him make the sign of submission on his forehead: the transporting of a mountain of metal was also the King's will, and as such must be done.

Luckily, though, the Salvans too have their dodges, although nothing to rival the Miners' machines: instead of carrying out the task immediately they followed Lois's advice and waited until winter, drinking nettle juice, like him, to keep themselves awake. Then, when the snows came, they dismantled the wheels of the ore-carts, replaced them by strips of wood, slighty curved at one end to prevent them from sticking in the snow, loaded the carts with the ore and slid them down the mountainside, two Salvans sitting on top of each load with their legs stretched out for braking and steering; down, down, until they reached the road that led to Fànes. It was rather like the game that the castle children used to play with the soldiers' shields. Once they met the road they climbed off the carts, hitched teams of dogs to them in place of horses (the horses, being heavier, would have got bogged down in so much snow), and made the rest of the journey that way, scampering along beside the yapping dogs.

The soldiers and the Miners, when they saw what was going on and what fun it was, asked if they could join in. They even organized races, cart against cart and team against team, and placed bets on one another, so that in the end the work was done in next to no time, and everyone was quite sorry when it was over.

I remember listening to the sound of their laughter as the carts set off – they laughed every single time in exactly the same way, Look at 'er! Look at 'im! Haw, haw, haw! – and thinking how silly it sounded. If I had known how long it would be before I heard the sound again of Fanes and Miners and Salvans laughing together, I might have appreciated it more.

CHAPTER EIGHT

Poison

 ois used to say that metal poisons men in their hearts as well as their skins. He blamed it for a lot of things. Everyone knows the blisters that the smiths get from the furnaces – well, according to him the same kind of damage happened to a man's heart when he lived too close to metal, or thought about it too much: his heart began to scorch. Metal made people greedy, he claimed, and greed made them hoard, and the hoards tempted other people to steal as never before. And when I pointed out that some people always *did* steal things – food, horses, anything they could get their hands on – he would smile his sad variety of smile at me and say, Ah, yes, Alexa, but they steal these kinds of things because they *need* them: metal they steal because they *want* it, it is rather different.

He may have been right about this, I don't really know. Like the business of Fate, I tend to think that metal is just metal and that we are the ones who turn it to good use or to bad. One thing is certain though: it was now that the ore lay above ground, and no longer quietly hidden beneath it, that the bad things started to happen. And they started very soon.

When the last of the ore-carts had slithered down the mountainside with its riders aboard, the Miners began packing up their belongings and preparing to return to their homes. They were quick about striking camp, as they were quick about most things, but when everything was almost packed and ready there was a sudden turn-about, and they began undoing all their bundles again and spreading their chattels about them, as if they'd had second thoughts about leaving.

I was upstairs with Tilly in the room where we stored the apples since the disaster with the ear-wigs, doing a morning food-check. We had a good view of the scene from the window. 'What do you think they're up to, Till?' I asked her. 'The Duke won't like it if they're still here when he gets back from hunting. He says he's fed up to the teeth with all their filth and noise.'

Tilly frowned, she agreed with the Duke on this point, said that the Miners' grit got everywhere and spoiled the wash. 'I don't know, poppet,' she shrugged. 'Looks to me like they're searching for something. They're always doing that – losing bits and pieces of their gear and accusing people of stealing them. I've never known workers so careless of their tools. Let's hope they find whatever it is soon and clear off, is all I can say.'

The time passed, however, and the shadows got shorter and then longer again, and the Miners were still there, busy rummaging. From inside the castle we could hear their voices getting louder and louder, more and more frenzied: 'Where's it got to? Who was in charge of it? Who saw it last? Mange on the idiot whoever he was!' Finally I went outside with old Hubert, who enjoyed fusses of this kind, to find out what the hitch was and whether we could give any help.

I am afraid I wasn't very tactful, but then it's hard to be tactful when people are so pig-headed. The Miners had lost something, of course, just as we thought, but they refused to say what it was. 'An object, Highness,' was all they kept repeating, raking and re-raking through their scattered belongings and turning them inside out and upside down until you wouldn't even have been able to find a cow amongst them, they were in such a mess. 'We have lost an object, a valuable object, an irreplaceable object. Oyoyoy! Oyoyoy!'

'I thought that was the noise you make when you find things,' I said shortly. I was already losing patience, because how can you help someone find something if they won't tell you what it is they have lost?

The Chief of the Miners stepped forward at this point, hammer in hand, and waved it under my nose. It was the highest he could reach. 'It's the noise we make to call our people together, Princess Busybody,' he said rudely, 'when we have something important to announce. And I am announcing something important now: a very special part of our equipment has gone missing, and we're not leaving here without it. No, no, and triple no. That old fellow now . . .' and he swung the hammer round to point at Hubert's chest, 'I bet he could tell us a thing or two about where it's got to. Don't think we haven't noticed you, you old greylocks, prying around the shafts at night, looking for pickings, pocketing our tools. Wouldn't be surprised if you'd nicked it yourself.'

There were ugly growly noises of agreement from the other Miners. Hubert, delighted to be the centre of so much attention, started growling back and clenching his fists and baring his two remaining teeth. It looked as if we might be on the brink of a big row.

I wouldn't have sworn to Hubert's innocence, to be quite honest: I'd seen a lot of Wanderers coming and going recently with heavy looking bundles, and I had a suspicion he'd been pedalling leftover bits of ore to them on the sly, like he did with the hay, but I couldn't very well say this to the Chief of the Miners, it would only have made him angrier.

Poison

'Please,' I said quickly, taking the little man by the hand without the hammer in it, and leading him aside where nobody could hear us. 'Let's be reasonable. We neither of us want it to come to a fight, do we? So let's make a deal. You pack up your things now and leave quietly, with or without your mysterious object, and I'll make a promise to you. You tell me what it is – just me, no one else – and I'll do my best to find it for you. I'll make enquiries, I'll leave no stone unturned. And then, when I've found it I will send it back. How does that sound?'

At the mention of stones the Miner Chief gave me a very shirty look. I was rather offended because up till then I had always thought he liked me. 'It sounds as if you're party to the theft, Highness,' he muttered. 'That's what it sounds like to me. How did you know it was a stone, otherwise?'

I had difficulty taking in his meaning. 'Oh,' I said after I'd done some rapid thinking, 'so it's a *stone* you have lost. It's a *stone* you're making all this fuss over, an ordinary old stone.' (I knew perfectly well it must be a special sort of stone he was alluding to – probably a jewel-stone: the Miners were said to have dozens of these in their possession, stashed away with their gold in their famous secret store-place of Aurona – but I thought it best to play stupid and pretend I didn't.) 'Well, there are plenty more available. Help yourself. Take another one. Take two. Take as many as you like. I'm sure nobody will mind.'

The Chief of the Miners looked hard into my eyes, and then scratched his head with the pointed part of the hammer. 'Roast me liquid if I don't trust you!' he said grudgingly after a few more scratches. 'I don't trust your father, and I don't trust the Duke, and I don't trust that scheming old hench-man of yours over there, rot his gums, but I trust you. Must be those eyes, they're clear as a summer sky. Very well, we'll do as you say, Princess – we'll leave right now, without making any more trouble. There's fat little to be gained by staying anyway: if the stone's lost it's well and truly lost, and if it's been stolen . . .'

'It's been well and falsely stolen,' I finished for him.

'Right,' he agreed, staring hard at me again, and not in the friendliest of fashions. 'Couldn't have put it better myself. Very neat, aren't we, with our words? But mind you stick to your part of the bargain, Princess Alexa, and look out for our stone for us. And mind you send it back if you find it, else we'll have it off you by force. We will do anything – *anything*, you understand,' and he brandished the hammer again, 'to get our hands on it. Remember that!'

I began to repeat, rather wearily at this point, that if he wanted me to find the stone, he'd better hurry up and tell me what the wretched thing looked like: at least what colour it was and what shape. But he cut me short and shook his head. 'Na, na, na,' he said, 'that's my little secret, my little safeguard. You'll recognize it all right if you see it. Oh, yes, you will. And if you don't, then I'd rather you didn't, if you get my meaning. I'd rather no one did.' Then he smiled and pulled down the corner of his eye with his finger. 'No description, your blue-eyed Highness, and no hints and no tip-offs either. Trust is good, as we say in Mill Brook, but mistrust is better.'

I blinked. I didn't have to feign stupidity this time, I really didn't understand a word. 'If that's the way you want it,' I said, and spread my hands. 'But I still don't see how I can recognize something if I don't know what . . .'

Quick as lightning the Miner Chief spat in his palm and took one of my hands in his: the bargain, such as it was, was sealed. 'That's the way I want it,' he confirmed. 'Clear pact, long friendship. We skedaddle, meek as sheep, and you send us the stone – when and if you come across it. Agreed?'

It still didn't seem a very clear pact to me, but I nodded and did my part of the spitting and left it at that. The Miners are touchy folk, it doesn't do to query their intelligence. Before sunset, and luckily well before the Duke returned, they had done as their Chief had promised and bundled their gear together for the second time that day and disappeared down the slopes, leaving nothing but the ashes of their fires behind them. They had even filled in the openings of the empty mine-shafts with earth, so that apart from the patches of freshly turned soil you would hardly have known they had been there at all.

'Good riddance to bad rubbish,' Duke Raymond commented when he got back. 'I hope they took their fleas as well.' But I don't think they can have done because we all of us scratched for days.

It looked now as if we were in for another stretch of boredom. Apart from the last little incident I had rather enjoyed the Miners' stay: their songs, their stories, the sense of danger that accompanied them by day as they set out to work, and the sense of cosiness and safety that hung over the camp at night, when they were all back and rested and accounted for. I thought I would miss them – I was sure Dola would, she'd become very pally with all the children in the camp and hardly ever left the place, only to sleep – but as things turned out we didn't have time.

Only a handful of days later I was woken in the night by the sound of shouting. More like wailing, really, than shouting. My nose for trouble must have been in working order by now, because I sensed disaster in the air immediately. I tore downstairs in my nightclothes, just a blanket over me against the cold, and was met at the bottom by the Commander of the Fànes guards. He was white with snow from head to foot; if I had believed in the return of the Unready Dead (which I don't think I do, or the night-world would be crowded with them, surely?), then that is what I would have taken him for: a wraith on the prowl. For a moment I hoped he might be on a routine visit – he did that sometimes now that my own guard had been withdrawn: just called by to see if Dola and I were well or needed anything – but one look at his face told me this was not so. It was white, a different white from the snow, but just as pale, just as ghostly.

'Be brave, Highness,' he said straight out, laying a freezing hand on my shoulder. 'Be strong. I bring terrible news from Fànes. Your parents – the King – the Queen – they are dead. We don't know how, we don't know why, whether it was a disease or a bane or something they ate by mistake, but they are dead in their beds, stiff as winter locusts already. Forgive me for being the messenger of such news.' And with this he let go of my shoulder and dropped to his knees in front of me and covered his head with his cloak.

I don't know what I felt at that moment. Plunged into darkness, I think, as if my own head was also shrouded. I couldn't say I had loved either of my parents, nor they me, but they had been there, in the background of my life – familiar and lasting and belonging, like a couple of pieces of rather hard but sturdy furniture. And now, if this dreadful news was to be believed, they were no more.

I bent down and uncovered the Commander's head for him and helped him to rise. He had plaits like my father, and they swung as he stood up, and on seeing this I was pierced by a shaft of sadness – or perhaps it was loneliness – so painful that it took my breath away. Faraway parents of mine, I begged silently, faraway parents, gone even farther now, why do you leave me like this? Come back, both of you, come back. I am not ready to carry this burden, not yet, not yet.

The full weight of the burden, however, had still to make itself felt. As we stood there, the Commander and I, looking at one another in silence across the light of the flare, wondering what to say next and which of us ought to say it, the Duke arrived and demanded to know what was going on. Or, as he put it with his usual grace, what the stinking, fuming pigswill was going on? He'd clobber whoever it was had dared to wake him in this fashion! And when he learnt the news I saw his face crease with a pleasure he was unable to conceal, and the Commander's face on the other side of the flare darken with just as much displeasure, and realized we were in for power struggles, possibly nasty ones and certainly very soon. The Duke would want the Kingdom of Fànes now, he would look on it as his right, and the Fanes would not want him for their King. This was a mountainload of worries on my shoulders straight away.

The next load was dropped shortly afterwards, when Muley, who had appeared quietly by my side at some point and was now holding my hand in a comforting way for which I was very grateful, began plying the Commander with questions. Who had found the bodies of the King and Queen? In what positions had they been lying? Had the Commander seen them with his own eyes? What food had they eaten for supper? Had they vomited? Had they called for help? How long had their agony lasted? Had anybody else been taken ill besides their Majesties? Questions like these, which I suppose I ought to have thought of asking myself but didn't.

Most of them remained without reply, because, as the Commander had said at the outset, nobody really knew very much about what had happened: my parents had gone to their beds in good health, had been taken suddenly ill in the night, and after a short but violent struggle against the illness, or whatever it was, had died. Just the two of them, as far as he knew. In a matter of finger-snaps. The Nurse had heard their groans and had run to their bedside, but they were dead by the time she reached them, and that was all there was to tell. When Muley insisted, however, and asked about the state of the room and whether anything strange had been noticed – anything missing, anything out of place, anything there that there shouldn't have been – the Commander's eyes lit up with sudden interest and he said, yes, wait a moment, it was lucky Muley should have mentioned that because there *had* been something odd about the room now he came to think of it: there had been a lot of dark gritty stuff on the floor and on the bedclothes, and one of the servants who had helped to lay out the corpses had found, clasped in the Queen's hand, a little black hammer. Now, how could the grit have got there when the room had been swept that very morning, and what could a person on the verge of death have possibly wanted with a hammer?

I had to cling tight to Muley's hand to prevent myself screaming. (Goodness, his hand was cold! Worse than the Commander's.) I didn't know either what a person on the verge of death could have wanted with a hammer, but I knew straight away, with a sick-making, flesh-creeping certainty, what the owner of the hammer had wanted from the persons on the verge of death: the stone, the mysterious stone, that was what he had wanted. My parents – somehow, I didn't know how and perhaps I never would now that they were no longer here to tell me – had come into possession of the Miners' stone, and the Miners had murdered them in order to get it back. What had their Chief said before he left? 'We will do anything, *anything* to get our hands on it!' At the time the words had had an almost comic ring about them, or so I had thought, but now I remembered them as evil, full of threat and malice. What was I to do, I wondered miserably? Oh, what was I to do? How could I expose the Miners' treachery without telling about the stone? I had sworn myself to silence, how could I go back on my word? And yet at the same time, how could I keep silent, when by my silence I was protecting my parents' murderers?

I was saved from my quandary by Muley, whose

mind, as always, seemed to be working that much faster and harder than anyone else's. He didn't seem to mind my grip on his hand, didn't even seem to notice it. 'I don't know about the rest of you,' he said, looking from me, to the Commander, to the Duke, and then back at me again, 'but grit and hammer spells a Miner to me. An angry Miner. Perhaps several angry Miners. What if our hot-tempered little friends were dissatisfied with the deal they made with the King? What if they wanted more metal than the share they had agreed on, and the King refused to give it to them? What if they crept into the King and Queen's bedroom and poured poison in their mouths as they slept – murdering them out of spite, out of greed? I don't want to stir up trouble between our peoples until we're sure, but it looks to me as if this is very likely what took place. I think we should set out for Fànes as soon as the weather permits and prevent anything worse happening.'

I said nothing, but nodded until I thought my head would fall off. The Commander agreed and looked at Muley with great admiration: 'I hadn't thought of it in that light,' he said, 'fool that I am, I hadn't thought of it in that light at all. For sure, it must have been the Miners. Who else? They are the only ones who know about the ore. They are the only ones, beside ourselves, who know how to work it. For sure it must have been them, the little black scoundrels.'

The Duke gave an angry wiggle of his belly and

said that he *had* thought of it in that light, straight away, but that if it was a murder, and if the Miners had committed it, then the last thing they would do, surely, was to leave a hammer on the scene of their crime? Might as well have dipped their seal in the victims' blood and left little seal-marks all over the place: We did it, we did it. Besides, what did they need a hammer for if the method they used was poison? To break open the bottle?

'True, Your Grace,' Muley said. 'Very well said, very well thought out. But a Miner is never without his hammer, no matter where he goes or what he does – not even when he goes a-poisoning. And maybe it was the Queen, not the Miner, who used it. Have you thought of that? We all know how clever she was, how quick-witted: maybe she wanted to use it for that very purpose: as a seal-mark, as a pointer. Not, We did it, we did it, but, They did it, they did it.'

If I had had any doubt left in my mind about what had happened, Muley's words got rid of it for me. I could just imagine the scene: my mother dying, and furious to be dying, thinking to herself with her last strength, 'How can I skewer the little brutes? How can I see they pay for it? Come here, Master smutty Miner, come close enough and I'll spoil your game for you, you'll see if I won't.' It made sense, it convinced me utterly. And Muley was right, there was only one thing to be done: we must set out for Fànes immediately, before worse things happened.

CHAPTER NINE

Snowbound

The rest of that night, and the morning after, and the day after, and the night after that and the day after that, and for so many days that we lost count, it snowed and snowed. Nobody could arrive, nobody could leave, not even the Commander, nothing could be done but wait. And then when it stopped snowing the road was blocked and we had to wait again – this time until the thaw came. And when the thaw came the avalanches started to fall – thud, roar, thud, one a day at least – and there was more waiting still. The Commander's plaits had grown a full thumbnail before we were able to set out for Fànes and my parents' graves.

I used this period of waiting in the strangest of ways. There I was, up to my ears in trouble: my mother and father were dead – murdered, poisoned – and I couldn't reach them, not even for their funeral. I had no doubt who their murderers were, but I couldn't reach them either, and didn't know what I would do to them if I did. The throne of Fànes was vacant; the future was as blank as the landscape outside; the present was a household of cooped-up, crochety, fidgety people, plotting and planning and eating and grumbling, and all of them wanting things – generally from me. Muley wanted to talk politics – in secret, just the two of us. Dola wanted comforting. The Duke wanted to know what had happened to his wedding suit and whether it could be let out with gussets so that he could wear it for his coronation. The Commander wanted me to tell the Duke to stuff his wedding suit down his gizzard, gussets and all, and that there would be no coronation, not for him. Tilly wanted to know what she was to do about the packing. And then the unpacking. And then the packing again. (Sonia was about the only person who didn't want anything, but I was worried about her all the same, and couldn't decide whether to leave her behind when we left for Fànes, or wake her, or take her with us in the chest, or what.) Problems, big and small, crowded in on me from every side. But was I bothered by them? Was I crushed? No, I wasn't even dented. I was unruffled as the fresh snow outside, happy as an otter in a flood. I was in love, you see. I had chosen this of all convenient moments to fall dottily, totally, blissfully in love.

Snowbound

It had happened suddenly, quite without warning. One morning, shortly after the Commander's arrival, we were sitting in the Council Chamber – the Duke, his secretary, myself and Lois, the Commander, Muley, plus Rhoda and a few of the other bossies – locked in our usual barren argument about what was to be done, when and if the snow would ever let up and allow us to do it. The room was lit by grease-lamps: it was too cold outside to remove the shutters, and so dark anyway that it wouldn't have made much difference if we had. A fire was going and a bowl of hot beer had been brought in, and everybody was jostling elbows and ladling the beer into their mugs and slopping it all over the place. I had my marten-lined cloak on – I was never out of it in winter – but I didn't really need it because the room was warm, almost stuffy. I felt heavy-headed and melancholy and fed up with the lot of them: love, for any of these fellow creatures of mine, couldn't have been further from my mind.

We were arguing, as far as I remember, about the Miners. Not about their guilt, because that was more or less the only thing we had all come to agree on, but about how they were to be punished, and on what scale. The Commander wanted us to punish all of them – gallop down to Mill Brook and round them up and hang a good number of them and set their huts ablaze and spike a few more and generally teach them a lesson they wouldn't quickly forget; while the Duke (who disliked my parents and, although he couldn't say so outright, was tickled pink with the Miners for what they had done) was more clement for the once. He wanted us to hang just a round dozen, six for each victim. I was silent most of the time because, although I knew revenge was right and a duty, I kept on thinking of the Miners and how nice they had seemed, and how we had sung songs together, and how their children had played with Dola, and how horrible it was to be sitting round a table now, discussing how many of them to kill.

Tempers were growing warmer than the room. The Commander was accusing the Duke of cowardice, the Duke was accusing the Commander of meddling, Rhoda was accusing me of being what she called a fish in a barrel (meaning, I think, that I was being slippery and not taking a firm position), Muley was keeping up a steady flow of abuse against the Miners to remind everyone, quite rightly I suppose, who our real enemies were. Whichever way I looked I saw flushed ugly faces, mouthing even uglier words: Chicken-heart! Blubber-liver! Prod-snout! Prod-snout yourself! Curse you! Curse *you*! Curse *them*! Rats! Vermin! Traitors! Then, I don't know why or what prompted me, but I looked under the table and saw Lois kneeling there in the half-darkness, and his face was so different, so still and peaceful and superior-looking, that I knew in that very instant that I loved him. Not like a friend, I mean, the way I had loved him up to then, but like a real lover.

It was quite extraordinary. The noise in the room stopped, my heart stopped beating. I hoped for their sake my parents were well and truly dead and their eyes burnt to cinders, because they would have died all over again of shame if they could have seen me. 'Lois,' I whispered. He wasn't looking at me, he was looking beyond me, his thoughts elsewhere. 'Lois! *Lois*! Come outside, quick, I have something to tell you.'

My idea, I think, was to confess my love to him on the spot. The way I told him everything: what to do, where to go, what to bring me, when to buzz off because I wanted to be alone. But it was a funny thing, once we were outside the room I suddenly felt frightened of him. Can you believe it? Me, frightened of my servant, my shadow?

I stood there in front of him, tongue-tied and clammy-handed (and slightly cross with myself as well, because I do not like fearing another person, whatever the reason). I was taller than he was, and I could see the top of his head where a small bald patch was beginning to form in his otherwise thick and glossy hair. This frightened me even more. So much time has passed already, I thought in panic, so much wasted time. What if I have left it too late? When he declared his love to me, all those years ago, I didn't bother to acknowledge it, didn't even say, Oh? or, Is that so? What if he does the same to me now? I know it would serve me right for being so blind, so arrogant, so foolish, but I just couldn't bear it, I just couldn't bear it!

Lois told me afterwards that he had half a mind to do exactly that: hear me out in silence and then say, Too bad, Alexa, come back in five years' time and we'll see. But he didn't, of course, because it wasn't too late and, little as I deserved it, he did still love me. He didn't say anything. And neither did I. We just stood there in the dim, cold, empty hall for what seemed a lifetime and no time at all, looking at one another, reading things from each other's eyes as if they had been picture books like this one I am writing. Then he opened his strong sinewy Salvan arms, which had once seemed so ugly to me and now seemed utterly beautiful, and I stepped into them and he closed them about me, and the lonely feeling I had felt since my parents' death vanished like a puddle in the sunshine. I felt happier than I had ever felt in my life. When we went back into the Council Chamber, as we did pretty smartly so as not to arouse suspicions, I had to keep covering my mouth with my cloak, I was so afraid my happiness would show.

From that moment on, and for many, many moon-cycles until habit wore down the barrier between them, I lived in two different worlds. The pretend world of daylight in which I was Duchess, Princess, housekeeper, mother, politician, ear-

piece, emblem, cushion between factions, and I
know not what; and the real world of night-time in
which I was just Alexa, Lois's lover. Our meetings
were dangerous, but simple to arrange. We would
wait until all was quiet in the castle and everyone
asleep, then Lois would creep out of his sheepskin
bag which lay outside my door, plump it up and
put a piece of rolled-up fur in the opening so that it
looked as if he was still inside it, and join me in my
bedroom. In my bed. And there he would stay
until early morning, when the flocking of the birds
warned us it was time for him to return to his usual
place, on the other side of the door.

I miss him so badly, even now, that I don't really
want to think back on what we did together in these
stolen nights of ours – many, I suppose, if I count
them, but far too few if I count the ones I've spent
alone. I don't want to remember the way he touched
me, the way he held me, the way he brought me
alive and took me in my head to places I never knew
existed and made flames leap inside me I never knew
burned. All I have left of him now is a claw I wear
round my neck on a chain, and I don't even look at
this very often if I can help it: it is dry and shrivelled
and has gone a funny colour, probably on account of
soaking it too long in the brine.

Of those first, dizzy-making days of our love affair
– the last we spent in Crow Mount – I doubt I could
remember much anyway, even if I tried. I went
around boss-eyed and dreamy, like the Shaman in

one of his trances, smiling at people, laughing for no reason, tripping over things. I expect Lois did too; I am surprised more people didn't notice. One of the few things I do recall, though, and that chiefly because of what happened afterwards, was a conversation we had on the morning we were leaving about the Miners, in which Lois made me promise, much against my will to begin with, to do everything I could to delay the punishment expedition. 'Stall,' he told me. 'Dig your toes in. Play for time. You say you *know* they're guilty, but you don't, you know. You think they're guilty, you *believe* they're guilty, you're even prepared to say you're sure they're guilty, but you don't know it, not the way you know we're here in this bed together. Wait until you know it like that, and then you can go ahead and think about punishment. Blood spills easy, Alexa, it's pouring it back into the body again that's difficult.'

Like his mother's saying about nothing being sure, this advice didn't seem particularly clever or helpful at the time, but I'm glad I listened to it all the same and made my promise. Whether I would have kept it is another question. I hope I would, I even think I would, but I shall never really know for certain (not by Lois's standards anyway) because by the time we reached Fànes it was too late for toe-digging or delay tactics of any kind: with the best intentions, but, alas, worst consequences, matters had been taken out of our hands.

CHAPTER TEN

Throwing Dice

muley had a story he used to tell Dola about some famous General or other crossing a river and playing a game of dice while he crossed and shouting out to his soldiers, 'I have cast the die'. I don't remember how it went or why it was supposed to be so interesting, but I know the point of it was to show that there are actions – like the throwing of a die presumably – that once done cannot be undone.

And Lois was right, the shedding of blood is one such action: you cannot pour shed blood back into the body again, and you cannot stem the flow of hatred that follows on the flow of blood. Powerless as a wet butterfly you are swept along by the current, and the current leads down, down, down, and whirls faster, faster, faster.

We set out for Fànes on one of the brightest and most beautiful days I have ever seen, leaving Rhoda to take care of things in our absence. A happy solution all round. My heart should have been heavy, but what with love and sun and homecoming it was light as a puffball. True, there were sad and difficult things still to do, like entering my parents' tomb to say goodbye to their ashes, and sorting out their left-over clothes and possessions, and deciding about revenge and the succession and what have you, but with Lois at my side at night to comfort me, and Muley in the daytime to give counsel, I felt I could cope with anything. I was coming back to where I belonged, to my own mountains, my own people. Not as their Queen, because Muley and I had already decided that the only tactful solution, acceptable to both the Fanes and the Duke, was for me to waive the crown and pass it on to Dolasilla, but as their Princess Regent. Which was every bit as good, perhaps better. A Princess Regent is not so grand as a Queen: I wouldn't have to sit around in my best clothes, sewing and yawning like my mother did, I could go out and about, take up my riding again, visit the wood-carver, the shepherds, perhaps even go as far as the Salvan highlands with Lois and try to catch a glimpse, just from a distance, of our borrowed daughter. The last heather-bound packet had contained a pair of shoes – 'See what care we take of her, Princess? We are not letting her go barefoot like us' – and they were intriguingly large with deeply scored toe marks.

Tilly was with us, I had insisted on that, much to Rhoda's pique, so apart from naughty old Hubert and Baldur and the birds, I was leaving behind me no one and nothing I really cared for. 'Travel light, woman, for fury's sake!' Duke Raymond had ordered when he saw my bundles – fine words, coming from someone who took up a whole cart to himself. But I had ignored the order and taken with me clothes, boots, jewellery, writing things, owl, donkey, the donkey harness, my heather-wrapped parcels, everything I possessed. Not to mention Sonia, tucked into Lois's sheepskin bag, and her chest, which I used as an extra packing case. I even took Dola's trousseau linen and all her toys, and my big hay mattress, because my Fànes mattress was too small for me and Lois together, and I couldn't bear the thought of us using the one my parents had died on. We had some trouble getting it down the crag to the road, I remember, it was so unwieldly, but in the end we used the Salvans' system and slid it on the last strips of melting snow.

Half way through our journey I had to stop and let the owl out of his travelling cage, he was making such a fuss. For a while he sat quietly on my shoulder, blinking, but it was only politeness, and after one or two hops and one or two sorties he was off, back to his old haunts. I called out to him

Good Luck, but the Duke glowered and said I should have had the wretched thing's wings clipped like he told me: only bad luck could come from losing an owl. And in this case I'm afraid he may have been right.

When we reached Fànes I think I could already tell that something was wrong. I hadn't expected cheering, the Duke was too unpopular and the King and Queen my parents too recently dead, but I had expected smiles, waves, some show of gladness at my return. Instead, faces in the courtyard when we entered were grim and voices were silent; the only beings who looked at all happy to see me were my father's dogs. Black crosses had been painted on the walls in sign of mourning and some of the castle folk wore them on their foreheads too. Others wore a red one. I didn't know what this signified – I was too young, I suppose, to have seen the sign before, and too lucky – but I was soon to find out.

Before I had time to step down from the cart the Deputy Commander came out to meet us carrying a large pair of baskets, rather like the ones we had used for the twins' ill-fated donkey ride, only rounder and with lids. A welcome ceremony of sorts. He wasn't smiling but his face wore the eager, look-what-I've-got-here-for-you expression of a hunting dog, bringing its master a rabbit. He said a few words – I picked out 'shame' and 'unbearable' and 'should have waited but couldn't' – and then placed the baskets on the ground, removed the lids, and with a symmetrical flourish of both hands fished out from each what I first took to be a couple of undersize pumpkins, badly rotted, but soon realized in horror were the heads of the Miner Chief and his wife. 'For you, Highness,' he announced proudly. 'And for the honour of all the Fanes. Revenge is taken. Welcome back to your troubled realm.'

There was an even deeper silence in the courtyard, broken only by the sound of Lois's fist crashing down in dismay on the wood of the cart (small wonder he was dismayed: if you can't pour back blood into the body, still less can you replace two severed heads), and a furious hiss of 'Cheeky underling!' at the Deputy from his Commander, who knew his thunder had been stolen. I covered Dola's eyes, but it was too late, she had seen everything. Then in the hush the Shaman stepped forward with his lyre at the ready, and in the solemn sing-song voice of grand occasions, interspersed with lots of strumming as he thought up his rhymes, began to explain to us what had happened.

'Our King was dead, our Queen was dead,' he sang, 'and we were left without a head. We wondered what we ought to do. We asked ourselves but no one knew.

'Our King was dead, our Queen was dead. We found a hammer in their bed. We found another underneath; a pick, a knife without a sheath.' (This was partly for the rhyme, of course: I found out later that the mining tools which had come to light after the Commander had left were in fact a second hammer, an axe, a chisel, and a hat with a candle in it, all found underneath the window and not underneath the bed as the song implied. I was glad about this find, because it furnished such strong proof of the Miners' guilt it silenced even Lois.)

'We knew our foe but couldn't reach him, Knew lessons that we couldn't teach him. All winter long we bore the shame. How to avenge our rulers' name?

'How to greet our dear Princess? With a wrong and no redress? Fanes are strong and Fanes are proud, Cowardice is not allowed. Fanes are proud and Fanes are strong, Never will they bear a wrong, for long.' (Either the Shaman's rhythm was at fault here, or else it is my memory, but this is the wording I remember.)

'Fanes are strong and Fanes are fell, The folk of Mill Brook know that well. On the very eve of spring, We went and killed their Miner King.

'Took his life and killed his wife, And tit for tat and end to strife. But Miners are not fair like Fanes, A darker blood runs through their veins.

'Not for them the reign of justice, Not for them the . . . um . . . um . . .'

The Shaman seemed to have run himself into deep rhyming difficulties here, and by now I was becoming so worried and impatient that I broke with ceremony and interrupted his song. I think it was the red crosses that opened my eyes. That, or the sight of a great crumbling breach in the wall opposite as if a giant mouth had taken a bite out of our masonry and spat it on the ground.

'It's war, isn't it?' I almost shouted at him. 'That's what you're trying to tell us. The Miners have declared war on us and have struck back already?'

The Shaman put his lyre on the ground and looked at it. Sadly, as if it were a living thing that was ill or had just died. 'Yes, Highness,' he mumbled. 'And no, Highness. The Miners have declared war on us, that is, but it was not them, unfortunately, but their allies the Cajutes who made the attack.'

I gasped. We all did, except for Muley who was looking strangely smug. The Cajutes? The lawless, godless, friendless Cajutes? Since when were the Cajutes allies of the Miners? Since when were they allies of anyone?

Without realizing, I must have asked this last question out loud, perhaps very loud. The Shaman shrugged unhappily and kept his eyes down. 'Who knows?' he said. 'Since they saw the colour of the Miners' gold, most like, or the glitter of their jewel stones. Allies can be bought if you pay a high enough price, and we have reason to think that's what the Miners are doing: parting with some of their precious stored-up treasure in exchange for the Cajutes' help in battle. So far they seem to be getting quite good value on the deal too, as you can see.' And he gestured towards the hole in the wall, through which I now noticed a stream of ash flecks was wafting: there'd evidently been more funerals of late, and goodness knows how many more to come.

'Who'd have thought the little varmints would take their punishment so hard,' he added, looking up at me now and allowing me to see the worry in his eyes. 'Who'd have thought they'd be so vindictive?'

Lois would have thought it, Lois *did* think it, I wanted to reply. But Lois's wisdom was of no use to any of us now, so I said nothing; merely stepped down from the cart, picked up the baskets so as not to appear ungrateful for this gruesome gift which had cost my people so much and was meant so well, and began to walk towards the castle entrance. Mud, war, destruction, and a brace of gory heads, I thought to myself as I went – what a homecoming. I told the Shaman later that I had thrown baskets and contents onto the pyre, but in fact I had Lois take them down to Mill Brook and leave them outside the wall. Not that the Miners deserved much consideration after what they had done, but it seemed to me that even to a wicked enemy like them some respect was due.

CHAPTER ELEVEN

Blond Iron

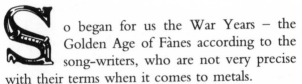o began for us the War Years – the Golden Age of Fànes according to the song-writers, who are not very precise with their terms when it comes to metals.

To start with, I must admit, there was little to show that we were entering a new phase of our history, golden or otherwise. War sounds a violent and uncontrollable thing, but in fact, as both sides waged it at the outset, it had its rules and its boundaries, and everybody knew them and kept to them. In the first place, full-scale battles were a spring affair and a spring affair only: in summer there was the harvest to be seen to, in autumn there was the drying and salting and preserving of food stocks, not to mention the hunting, and in winter – well, in winter there was the snow, full-stop.

Second, even in the right season, battles couldn't be fought very often: weapons blunted easily, armour dented, and after each clash there had perforce to be a rest period while everybody sharpened up their points again and hammered out their dents. Third and most important, rather like in dog-fights or squabbles between other animals, it was the show that counted, more than the actual amount of damage inflicted. If one side could rustle up enough punch, that is, and cause its opponent to waver, even for a moment, or flinch, or lose ground, or lose heart, then that was it: irrespective of the count of dead or wounded (and often this point was reached so quickly that there were neither), the battle was considered over. The winning side would gather together and bang their shields and blow their horns, and the losers would shuffle off in silence, looking – and feeling – ashamed, and there the matter would end until the next encounter.

The first year, and most of the second, we waged war according to these rules. Neatly, rhythmically, almost like partners coming to-gether to dance. We lost five soldiers all told – one in combat and four afterwards from arrow-wounds gone septic – and the Cajutes, who had no Shaman to foist smelly ointments on them made of wax and goat pee, even fewer. It was that sort of a business: rowdy, blustery, only a titch more dangerous than hunting.

In midsummer, when the first round of combats stopped, Dolasilla was crowned Infant Queen of All the Fanes. It was a beautiful ceremony, although I ought not perhaps to say this seeing that I organized it myself. It took place on the top of the sunniest and friendliest of the Friendly Mountains, the one that used to be called Heather-top but is now known as Plan de Corones, or Coronation Field. People came from miles around and basked in the sunshine and ate and drank and stared and cheered and sang, and talked about nothing else for seasons afterwards. Mindful of my wedding, I tried for Dola's sake to make everything as different as possible, and except for the drunkenness at the end I think I succeeded: no one can stop Fanes getting pie-eyed on a feast day, it's part of the fun. There were flowers, bells, flutes, cymbals, obligatory baths and clean clothes for everyone. The food was well cooked and there was plenty of it. The Duke, beyond the aid of gussets, wore a new suit of green which matched his face: he tried not to show it but he was peeved sick at being made a paltry Prince Regent while his eight-year-old daughter became Queen. The Shaman looked imposing, from a distance, in a long orange cloak embroidered with what Tilly had intended to be comets but had come off her needle as tadpoles. Dola, splendid and beautiful as a real comet, wore white trimmed with jay's feathers and her dress had a train so long it took six handmaidens to carry it. My father's crown was too big for her, so we had a new one made: a plain circle of copper, studded in the front with a single crystal the size of a crab apple, which had been found in my mother's jewel casket after her death. (I had a nasty feeling when I saw it that it might be the Miners' stone – the one all the fuss was about and that I had promised to return to them if ever I found it. But I couldn't be sure, and quite frankly, seeing how faithless the Miners had been themselves, I couldn't be bothered either. It was beautiful, and it was ours now, and that was that.) When the Shaman placed it on Dola's head the sun shone through the stone and sent out a multicoloured ray like a rainbow, and everyone went Iiiih! and Ciara! – look at that! – and took it as a sign of great things in store. Raietta! they shouted, A little ray. Fortunae müda!

And our fortunes were indeed on the change. The first change I noticed myself, however, was in Dola, and it was not a change I liked. Anything but. I don't know to this day what went wrong, whether, like I said, we had spoilt her already, or whether it was her new importance that went to her head, or whether, as she herself told me much later on, she had found out about my closeness with Lois and resented it, but from the moment the crown was placed on her head she was a different person. Critical, aloof, scathing, impatient; never with a moment to spare for me, always running off to Muley in his turret on the excuse that they had work to do together. She was cleverer than I was, of course – better educated too – but the division went deeper than that and cut more bitterly. We no longer seemed to share the same likes and dislikes, the same way of looking at things, indeed it sometimes felt to me as if we were strangers from two distant valleys, hardly able to understand each other at all. As a coronation present I gave her my ponies, all except one, hoping she would become fond of them and come out for rides with me, but she rode them in the courtyard instead with the Duke, training them to dodge and swerve and jump and spin on their haunches; schooling them for battle. I gave her my toys too – my carving kit, my set of knucklebones, my chequers; she said thank you, Alexa, as if talking to a halfwit (she always called me Alexa now), and stowed them away in a chest as soon as my back was turned. She was never openly rude to me, never churlish or disobedient; she just veered away on her own course leaving me as far behind as she could.

War seemed to be her favourite game, her only game. War and everything connected with war, from weapons, to shields, to tactics, to fortifications and earth works and I know not what. She and Muley must have learnt a lot of things of this kind from the Miners, because the pair of them seemed to know twice as much already as anyone else in the castle, and that first winter in Fànes they talked and busied themselves about almost nothing else. The Duke was thrilled, he followed them around like a dog, not understanding but barking enthusiastically all the same.

Outside the walls, in the secret hollow where the metal ore was stored, a smelting oven was built to Muley's specifications: he had pictures of it already drawn which he must have either copied from somewhere or thought up out of his own head. When it was finished it was quite different from the makeshift ovens the Miners had used for testing, far bigger and with much thicker walls, and when I remarked on this Muley said it was no mistake but as it should be. 'We want the ore to get much hotter than theirs did, Highness, you see,' he explained. 'Hotter and runnier.'

'Why?' I asked. Not that I wanted to know all that badly, but it seemed rude not to show interest.

'Aha!' he said mysteriously in his sweetest voice, and winked at Dola: he was just as much her friend now as mine, if not more. 'That's our secret. We just do.'

'Aha!' echoed the Duke just to annoy me. 'That's our secret.'

If it was a secret, however, what with the roar of the furnace and the ringing of the smithy and the shouts and the hammering of the smiths, it was not the sort that could be kept for long. Very soon the castle was buzzing with the news: Muley had found a new way of making iron. Not only smelting it and beating it into shape, like we had done before, but cleansing it and working it and making it into bars, harder and stronger than any that had yet been forged.

Dola, in a rare mood of friendliness, took me to see what was going on and explained to me the cause of all the excitement. 'He's been trying all winter,' she said, pointing at Muley, who was hopping round the floor of the smithy on one leg; not in triumph as it turned out but because he had burnt his foot on a piece of uncooled metal. 'He's been trying and trying, poor man, but there was always something that went wrong. First it was the oven that lost too much heat. Then it was the wood that burnt too fast. Then, when we replaced the wood by charcoal, it was the oven again, only this time it got too hot and nearly burst. Then it was the bloom . . .'

'The bloom?' I said. I was surprised Muley had used flowers in his recipe, the fiery blob of metal the smiths were pounding at with their rods didn't look that sort of a substance to me at all. 'What did you need blooms for?'

Dola tugged at my hand and laughed, for a moment she was almost like her old self again. 'Silly,' she said. 'The bloom is what the molten iron is called when it starts to harden. See that lump they're working on now? That's the bloom. It's got to be clean, you understand, free of impurities. The least little speck of stone or dust, and when you start working it, snap! it breaks like a wish-bone. Muley found this out, *and* found out how to deal with it. We hardly get any breakages now. Look how many arrowheads have been made today – dozens, scores. And look at the scrap-heap, how many have been lost: only a handful, and we can melt those down and roll them out again, like the creatures in the kitchen do with pastry.'

The creatures in the kitchen. Sonia's people, Lois's people. Perhaps, if Lulu and Dola were Lois's daughters, as he and I always liked to think they were, her own people. I felt my face grow hot, and it wasn't from the heat of the forge. 'The creatures in the kitchen, as you call them, are Salvans,' I reminded her sharply. 'They come from a brave, proud race, far older than ours. They deserve your respect.'

Dola smiled briefly and nodded; I doubt she was even listening. The whites of her eyes were dark as amber in the glow of the furnace, and for a moment I thought I saw them kindle with the same strange-coloured flash I had seen once in Muley's, that day by the Miners' fireside. 'The difficult part, of course,' she went on, talking more to herself now than to me, 'will come when we start on the blades and the shields. Flat things shiver even easier. But Muley has another pastry-cook's trick up his sleeve to deal with that. Haven't you, Muley? Come over here and tell us.'

Muley hopped obligingly closer, almost as if Dola had been holding him on a string. 'Welcome to our workshop, Highness,' he greeted me, friendly and smiley as ever. 'It's nice to see you taking an interest in metallurgy.'

My eyebrows went up in enquiry before I could stop them. He and Dola were always using long, difficult words which shut other people out of the conversation. 'Me-tal-lur-gy,' he repeated slowly in four parts for my benefit. 'The art of metal-working. Has her Little Majesty explained what we are up to? We're making something very, very special. Here, your Highness, take a look at this,' and he picked up one of the newly forged arrowheads and placed it in the palm of my hand. 'Feel it,' he said. 'Put your finger on the point and press.'

I did so, and watched, amazed, as the flesh of my finger parted with no pain at all and a gush of blood welled out. The new arrowhead was harder than a rock, sharper than a thorn.

'Oops! Careful!' Muley said, a little late to my way of thinking. 'Well, and what does our beautiful Princess Regent say to that? Better than bronze, no? Better than anything we had before?'

I was about to agree with him, but then looked at the blood still flowing from my finger and thought again. Weapons like these were better for those who hurled them; to those on the receiving end they would probably seem a great deal worse. 'I don't know about better,' I said slowly. 'Different, definitely.'

Muley took my finger and put it into my mouth for me and told me to suck it till it stopped bleeding and on no account show it to the Shaman. It was nice to see he still cared. 'Your Highness is worrying about the rust,' he said. 'I know, that's always been the problem with iron: the rust, the crumbling. But this time it won't happen. See how different the colour of this arrowhead is? Not black, not brown, but bright as silver? This is blond iron, Highness, as different from black iron as . . .'

'As Fanes are from Salvans,' Dola chipped in, quick as a lizard. I could have slapped her, but didn't because Muley already had that blank look on his face which he wore when he was being extra attentive. Besides, you can't really slap a Queen in public, no matter how small or naughty.

'As day is from night,' he continued smoothly as if he hadn't heard. 'Or as milk is from ink. And when it comes to the swords and shields, then, as her Little Majesty says, we're going to proceed like pastry-cooks and roll the iron out into sheets as thin as wafers, and pack the sheets together and bake them again, and so on, roll and bake and roll and bake, until we have a sheet that looks as if it's just one fine layer of metal but is in fact composed of dozens.'

I couldn't see the point of this at all. 'But pastry-cooks layer their pastry to make it softer, surely, not harder,' I said.

'Similies!' laughed Muley, and this time I kept my eyebrows level, even though the word meant nothing to me. 'See how they mislead us. Layered *pastry* gets softer, dear Highness, but layered *iron* gets harder. Much, *much* harder. Wait till we have some to show you. You'll be surprised.'

The baking method Muley described so blithely must in fact have been very difficult to carry out, because the new swords and shields were not ready for use until well into the spring, after we had already fought several battles with the Cajutes and were more or less preparing to put aside our arms for the season. (The new arrowheads *were* ready, of course, by the hundred, but shot arrows have a way of coming back at you, and it would have been foolish to use them before our soldiers had suitable protection.)

The soldiers were mistrustful to begin with, as they were of all novelties. A Changing of the Gear ceremony was held in the courtyard, presided over by the Shaman, in which each warrior was supposed to hand in his old fighting tackle and withdraw the new equipment in its stead, but it didn't work out that way at all. It was more like 'Donz' day, when the toothpuller did his yearly round: everyone protesting and clasping tight to what they'd got and refusing to part with it. Only this time it was weapons and not teeth. The Commander, who was meant to go first and set an example, put his sword on the ground with his shield on top of it, and sat down on both, glaring and snarling, like a dog with a bone. 'Come and get 'em,' he shouted at the poor Shaman, who was not famous for his daring. 'Come and get 'em if you want 'em. I'm not giving up good arms for those tin fripperies there. Needles and thimbles, that's what they are: better fit for sewing!'

The description caught on. 'Needles and thimbles!' the other soldiers started chanting, beating their old weapons together in rhythm, one-two-three-*four*-five, one-two-three-*four*-five. 'Needles and thimbles! Needles and thimbles! Smash them to pieces! We do not want them!' The noise was deafening.

The Shaman waved his hands about, trying to restore silence. He took a couple of steps towards the Commander and then drew back again, towards the platform where Dola and I and the Duke (beg his pardon, Prince Regent) were sitting, as a gob of spit landed close to his sandals. The chanting continued, stronger than ever. It was rather like a game of chequers when you get into a position where neither side can move: one small row of royal pieces confronted by a mass of pawns, and the shining armour lying like wager-counters in the middle of the board.

'Hey!' I saw rather than heard the Shaman whisper urgently in my direction out of the corner of his mouth. 'What am I to do? Think of something, quick, or we'll never win them round!'

I already was thinking hard but it was Dola who found a solution first. Stepping very slowly, very delicately down from the platform, with her skirts held between thumb and forefinger just as a Queen's should be, she made straight for the gleaming pile of weaponry and selected from it a shield, which she dragged, rather than carried, back to the platform again.

None of the soldiers moved to help her, suspecting a trick, I suppose, but by the time she was back in her place again the whole assembly had fallen silent out of sheer curiosity. I wasn't curious myself, I was horrified, because I knew exactly what she had in mind: with a time-lapse of about a hundredth part of a sand-glass, it was what I'd thought of doing myself.

'Fanes,' she announced in her small, shrill voice which sounded so tender until you heard the words. 'If these are sewing materials, as you say, then with them we will sew shrouds for the Cajutes, and for whoever else dares challenge us in battle. Shrouds, you understand; winding sheets; jackets for the dead. Come here,' and she did her string-pulling stunt on the Commander, who abandoned his weapons and advanced towards her meek as a tiddler on the hook. 'You have a good strong arm, hold this shield upright. Now, I will tell you all what I am going to do: I am going to stand behind this shield while your Commander holds it, and the strongest man amongst you is to come forward – with his *old* sword, mind you, not one of the new ones – and try to run me through. If he succeeds, not in wounding me because there's no chance of that, but in so much as scratching me, you can keep your old weapons: if not, then you give them up on the spot. What do you say to that?'

There was an incredulous silence, then one of the oldest soldiers stepped forward and, after a certain amount of throat-clearing and picking at his sleeve, began to speak. 'That sounds fair enough, Little Majesty,' he said, 'but it isn't, not really, because you know we can't allow it. If it was someone else now – the Prince Regent, for example, or . . . or . . . or the Prince Regent – it would be a different matter, but we can't any of us draw a sword on our own Queen.'

If I hadn't been so worried for Dola I would have started to enjoy myself: the Regent had been so boastful recently about the new equipment, and so scathing about what he called the Fanes' lack of enterprise, but now he was looking distinctly unenterprising himself. 'Ach! Prrh! Psss!' he began to splutter, glancing around him nervously and shifting his weight from one half of his backside to the other. 'What impudence! Their Regent, if you please! Why not use a pig? Just as good, if you ask me.'

Luckily nobody but me and Lois heard this remark, or things might have got really out of control. Lois nearly choked laughing as it was. 'The old porker's right, though,' he whispered when he could trust himself to speak again. 'It doesn't have to be a person. That's just Dolasilla being brave. It doesn't even have to be a poor pig either: a sack of beans is all we need.'

So in the end that was what was used: a sackful of last year's dried beans. And in the end of course, from tense and serious conflict between wills, the arms-test turned into a kind of game. Challenger after challenger hurled himself against the shield; sword after sword splintered and bent; the beans remained intact in their bag, no spillage, not even a dent. 'Magic beans!' the soldiers shouted at first, but it wasn't long before they were shouting, 'Magic shields!' and sidling over to the heap of armour to take one for themselves. After a while the Commander had to get some-one else to take his place, his arm had gone so wobbly from the effort of holding firm. Then the shield was changed, because each soldier was keen to try the one he had chosen. Then the pro-cedure was reversed and the beans were placed behind an old shield and charged at with the new swords, and this time it was the shield that splintered, and beans and bits of metal flew everywhere.

I looked at Dola, sitting quietly beside me now, watching the goings-on with a smile of rapt happiness on her face, and almost envied her. How strong she is, I thought to myself, how straight and pure; like a piece of blond iron herself. My own head was full of confusion. The atmosphere in the courtyard was playful, almost jubilant, and with reason: Muley had indeed made a great discovery with this new pale metal which slit through the bronze and leather shields as if they were so many cheese rinds. But I was unable to rejoice along with the others. I kept thinking what would happen on the day the blond iron would be used, not in make-believe combat as it was now, but in earnest, on the battlefield, against people like (or not so very *un*like) ourselves. It would not be beans strewing the ground then.

Were these traitor's thoughts? I supposed they were. Or if not traitor's thoughts, jinx's thoughts, unlucky thoughts, thoughts I should not have had. I slid my hand under the folds of my skirt so that nobody could see and sought for Lois's hand to hold on to. He, the outsider, the Salvan, was the only person I could confess such feelings to, the only person who would understand. 'I don't like it,' I whispered, not really knowing if by 'it' I meant the blond iron or the game or the situation or what. 'I don't like it one bit.'

Lois squeezed my hand and gave a tiny, almost unnoticeable smile. 'No more do I,' he whispered back. 'It's a right drunkard's nightmare. But there's no stopping it now.'

CHAPTER TWELVE

Eaglet

The battle of Mantena. Our first great victory, our first triumph of arms. In the songs it is called the Field of Dawn, the Starbirth, the Sunrise of our people, and other names, all having to do with light and beginnings. Fine words.

I didn't take part in the fighting this time, I was pregnant again and fortunately it was not expected of me, but I walked over the field of combat when it was all over, to inspect the damage and help tend the wounded, and of light and beginnings, I assure you, I found not a trace. On the contrary, I found long evening shadows, and black-beaked carrion crows squabbling over morsels, and death and destruction on such a scale that even we, the Fanes, the victors, were appalled by it. By what we had brought about.

'Wàswara?' I remember one of the wounded Cajutes kept repeating, staring at me and tugging urgently at the arrow that protruded from his thigh. 'Wàswara? Wàswara klept ons?' I thought he was asking for help to get the shaft out, but Muley told me afterwards the words meant, What is it? What hit us? The poor man was evidently in the grip of a curiosity stronger than his pain: he wanted to see the arrowhead, learn what this terrible new weapon was that had mown down his fellow warriors like corn stalks under the scythe.

The question – and all kinds of answers to it, from fanciful to fantastic – was soon going the rounds of the valleys and coming back to us via the Wanderers. (Who were almost too scared to come within our walls now, poor things, and did their commerce with us in whispers, through the chinks.) What was the secret of the Fanes' new-found power? A sorcerer. They had a sorcerer at their court, a powerful and terrible magician – half man, half mule. It was he, with his kicking hooves and biting teeth, who had won the day against the Cajutes. There was no withstanding him, no killing him: he was already dead, a wraith from the underworld with no flesh on his bones at all, just the skeleton which rattled when he fought. They had a Warrior Queen too with a star on her forehead; it was not the kicking mule but the ray of this star that had done for the Cajutes: it blinded anyone who looked at it. The sorcerer had made a magic shield for the Queen, and a dozen-and-one magic arrows, and with these she could slay an entire army in less time than it took to cook a pudding – the arrows never missed their target and flew straight back into her quiver after each shot. What with ray and shield and arrows, the Queen was invincible. And what with Queen and mule and magic, the Fanes were invincible. Unless they were stopped they would conquer the whole world, make prisoners of all the free tribes and have them slave and carry for them like the wretched Pack Salvans.

I doubt these stories were believed by everyone: it was common knowledge, for instance, that Muley, being a thinker and not a doer, never so much as showed his face on the battlefield, let alone his teeth or his imaginary hooves. But the gist of the stories, namely that the Fanes were getting too big for their boots by far, was certainly believed. And feared, worse than an outbreak of the cheese sickness. There was no more fighting that year, the Cajutes had no heart for it, but the next year and the next and the next again (and perhaps even a fourth or a fifth: the war years are so alike in my memory I almost lose count of them), we did nothing but stave off one attack after another.

On my insistence, we sent messengers to all the local chieftains, trying to reassure them, promising we had no quarrel to pick with anyone, but it was useless: our enemies grew in numbers, rapidly, like mushrooms after rain. The Lastojeres, the Peleghetes, the Latrones, the Cadubrenes – all the neighbouring peoples who had once been our friends and had traded with us and sent gifts for Dola's coronation – teamed up with the Cajutes and rode against us. The old rules no longer applied, neither as regards seasons nor anything else, and from the first signs of spring to the last falling leaves of autumn hardly a fortnight passed without our having to engage in some sort of military action. It became almost a way of life. For us, that is: for our opponents, cringing behind their old bronze and leather shields, with their crumbly black swords in their hands, it was closer to a way of death.

My son was born to the sound of battle-cries, and cut his first tooth to the same harsh music. Perhaps that – the noise, I mean, the sound of anger in the air – was the reason for his deformity, because he was born without a right arm; all he had in its place was a stump with a tiny pink hand attached, small and shiny as a twig of coral. I thought he was beautiful, stump and twig and all. He was dark, with round blue eyes and a smile no one could resist. The Regent wanted him called Raymond, but changed his mind when he heard about the missing arm, so I called him Eaglet instead, in memory of my dead brother, the would-be bird.

At least, I told myself, this one will not be a warrior when he grows up – how can he be, with only one arm? And I did everything I could to rear him differently, looking after him myself with the sole help of Sonia, teaching him to love music and birdsong and gentle manners, and keeping him as far as possible out of the clutches of the Regent and Muley and Dolasilla. The castle split gradually into two different camps as a result of these man-oeuvres, and I found myself living more and more like an outcast in my own home: cold-shouldered, disapproved of, treated by all except my closest associates as an oddity and a source of shame. One camp was huge and powerful and successful and included almost everybody; the other was tiny and was made up of me, Eaglet, Tilly, Lois and Sonia (and possibly the kitchen Salvans, had they been asked, and my old blind friend the vegetable-peeler), and that was about it. Nurse, funnily enough, came over to our side after a while, but I think that was just because she couldn't bear being without a baby. Muley shuttled between camps – a suave and always good tempered ambassador.

Dola was still too young to govern, the Regent was as unpopular as ever, and I was therefore, even now in my semi-disgrace, the person whom the Fanes looked on as their ruler and brought their problems to. (*And*, I may add, the person who had to wear the dreadful stuffy head-dress and make all the hard decisions.) But even with the head-dress in place, I was an unconvincing leader to most of them. They had put their hopes in me, but apart from Dola I had given them nothing to their way of thinking. No stirring speeches, no thanks for their valour, no encouragement. Where was I during the battles? Hidden away somewhere, crooning nonsense to my child, when I should have been taking him up to the look-out tower with the other children and showing him what life was all about. Where was I afterwards when the celebrations started? Out on the battlefield with the crows, talking to our enemies – those few that had any talk left in them; helping the wretches, bringing them water, dressing their wounds. It wasn't right for a ruler – that sort of thing should be left to menials. Anyone would have thought *we* were the aggressors from the way I went on, instead of the target of other folks' aggression. And talking of aggression, why wouldn't I let our soldiers pass to the attack now, the way Mulebones and the Commander urged we should, and wage a proper campaign of conquest with sieges and sackings and burnings and all the other tricks? Half measures were no good in warfare; you wanted to lam into the enemy, kick him when he was down and make sure he stayed that way. Any fool could tell you that; but me, no, I went on shilly-shallying and blathering about defence being better. Better for who? And whose side was I on anyway? Worst of

all, what had I done on the day my daughter slew
her first victim? Disgraced everyone, that was
what. Not only by refusing to blood the little
Queen's forehead with the mistletoe to bring
her luck in her next engagement, but by not
allowing the Shaman to do it either. It hadn't
mattered, because, blooded or not, Queen Dolasilla went from strength to strength, bless her tiny
spurs, but it was a shocking way for a Fanish ruler
to behave.

I knew this was what my people said about me. I
knew they found me strange and disappointing and
were beginning to look on me as a coward. (Lucky
no one ever came across me with my head in the
linen chest, or they'd probably have thought me
dotty as well and deposed me on the spot.)
However, I could do nothing to change the way
I was. Death, wounds, pain, combat – these things
didn't frighten me, they mystified me. Dola, in the
days we were still friends and spoke of such
matters, had told me once about the famous
Warrior's Thrill, of how the blood goes to the
head the way it does during the chase, making it
clear and befuddled at the same time, and how
nothing matters in those moments but victory and
the feel of your own strength meeting that of
others and overcoming it. As far as I was concerned she might have been speaking Salvan. No,
not Salvan, because thanks to Lois I was beginning
to understand that language, but some other

tongue – totally foreign, totally without meaning for me. What thrill could there be in slaying another being, and not even for the food? What pride in quenching another life? I couldn't fathom it, can't even to this day. Perhaps, as Muley said when I asked him about it, the Sun God, when he made me, forgot to put rennet in my heart, the way he does with most people, and as a result my heart was too soft. Or perhaps it was some other ingredient he forgot. Anyway, there I was at the head of my warrior people, as out-of-place and conspicuous as a black sheep among the white, or, the other way round, as a white crow among the black. A rarity. A freak. A mistake.

'Like Eaglet, you mean?' I remember asking Muley, to make sure I had understood about the rennet. 'Like him with his stump, I've got a piece missing which makes me unfit for warfare?'

And I remember too the way Muley laughed – sort of sorry and amused at the same time – and shook his head. Puzzling me until, a little later on, I discovered the reason. 'Yes to the last part, Highness,' he had replied. 'But no, not like Eaglet, not like Eaglet at all.'

How right Muley was. Hard though I tried to keep him away from it, and hampered though he was by his build, Eaglet inclined in his heart towards the other camp – to the side of the fighters, and it wasn't long before they claimed him. On the evening of his fifth birthday I went into his bedroom to say goodnight, to find him clad in battle dress from head to foot, already practising his strokes on the cloth bear that had been my present to him. He had lopped the animal's arm off (to make the contest equal, I presume) and ripped its stomach open so that all the stuffing had fallen out, and was now in the process of gouging out the embroidered eyes with the speed and lightness of a born swordsman. Flick, slice, flick, and away: the touch was so light that the material under the stitches was scarcely grazed. I didn't know whether to applaud or cry.

It was a conspiracy, of course, and they were all in it together: Dola, Muley, the Regent, the smiths, the soldiers; even Nurse, who confessed under pressure that instead of taking Eaglet for his walks she had been accompanying him each day to the forge to get the measurements right for the armour. ('Did I do wrong, Highness? Queen Dolasilla was so insistent. And he *does* look so sweet in it, doesn't he, bless his heart!' No, you silly woman, I felt like replying. You didn't do wrong. And think how sweet he will look on the battlefield – five years old, among the carnage.)

They had thought of everything, had answers to all my objections. He couldn't ride to battle like a Prince should? Nonsense, Dola had schooled a pony specially for him that obeyed foot commands. Eaglet's reins would be hooked to the saddle – a saddle with a hook on it was already being run up

for him – and all he'd have to do was to sit there
and use his legs and he'd be away in a blizzard. He
was too young? What, at five? Five was a perfectly
reasonable age to start soldiering. For the first year
or so he'd be behind the lines anyway, out of
arrow-shot, in the safe patch with the reserves. He
was lopsided, would lose his balance when he
swiped? Wrong. You only had to watch the
masterly way he wielded his birthday sword –
loose wrist, firm elbow, steady as an old timer
already. He couldn't use a shield? Never would be
able to? Ah! (they had been waiting for that one).
Not a normal shield, maybe, and not unaided; but
with the new fixed shield that Muley had invented,
which was buckled to the waist and not carried,
and with a shield-bearer at hand to tilt it for him,
he'd be able to manage just as well as everyone else,
if not better.

They even had a shield-bearer, if you please.
Trained and ready. A young man from the neutral
tribe of the Duranns, so nimble and sharp-sighted
that he had earned himself the nickname of Ey de
Net, or Eye of Night, due to his alleged ability to
see things in the dark. (They didn't of course
know, any of them, what they were taking on
with Ey de Net. But then neither did I, so I can't
say I drew much comfort from his presence at this
stage, rather the opposite.) They had a new bedroom prepared, for Eaglet and Ey de Net to sleep
in together. 'It's high time, Madam,' the Regent

snapped before I could start objecting to this as well, 'that our son kept the company of people of his own kind. He needs men around him, not just silly women and furry-wurries.'

Now, had it been just the conspiracy I was up against, these arguments I would have squashed like bed bugs, using as many fallacies, or whatever they were called, as I pleased. I would have smashed the horrid little suit of armour to smithereens for a start. Or, failing that (and no doubt I *would* have failed, because it was made, needless to say, of the very best and blondest iron), I would have thrown it into the river as an offering to the Eel God. I would have snapped back at the Regent, forbidden Dola and Muley my chambers, done anything – built a wall round my son, even – to prevent him leaving me and going over to the war-mongers. But it was not just the conspiracy, nor just the conspirators; it was Eaglet himself. I knew the moment I saw him with the bear, indeed perhaps I had known all along but hadn't wanted to admit it.

You see, I haven't quite finished saying what happened on the evening of his birthday. I said I stood there, not knowing whether to clap or cry. Well, in the end I did neither, just picked up the wrecked bear and asked Eaglet why he had requested this particular present if he didn't like it.

'But I *do* like it,' he said, hugging the bear close and kissing the sockets where the eyes had been. 'I love it. Can you heal it for me so it can play with me again?'

'The same game?' I asked in my sternest, most scornful voice. I had taught him dozens of games, scores, from knucklebones to chequers to tiddly-winks and hide-and-seek and I know not what.

He looked up in surprise. Offended, as if I had punished him for no reason. 'Of course,' he said. 'What other game is there?'

After that – those five simple words that said more than any book, or song, or speech, be it ever so long – I knew it was only a question of time before I lost him too, the way I seemed to lose all my children. The next day, therefore, I allowed Dola to move him into his new quarters, and watched, unprotesting, as she and Muley took over his education. Figures, fallacies, fencing, feinting, fighting, the lot.

I mended the bear, though, and noticed with relief that Eaglet seemed to have changed his mind about its function. When I peeped into his room a few days later to see how he was settling in, there it was, all in one piece, held tight against his cheek while he slept. It looked very out of place and childish in the big soldier's bed. But then so did Eaglet, and yet that was where by nature he belonged.

CHAPTER THIRTEEN

Rumours and Doubts

t was about this time, the time of Eaglet's transfer to the warrior camp and the arrival of Ey de Net, that I first began hearing talk of Aurona and the Miners' famous store of gold.

I had heard about it before, of course – everyone had. It was a byword for everything rich and sumptuous. 'Not for all the gold in Aurona,' Nurse had always used to say when there was something she didn't want to do; she said it still. 'Who do you think I am, the Queen of Aurona?' mothers would say to their children when they asked for things they couldn't have; or, 'We're not living in Aurona, you know, where the gold grows underfoot.' But now I began to hear it mentioned in a different way, as if it was a real place and as if somebody – it wasn't quite clear who, but I could make a guess – had a real intention of getting there and laying his pudgy hands on the treasure.

The castle children even began singing a song about it which they used for their skipping contests. Aurona wasn't mentioned by name in the verses, but it was easy enough to recognize from the description of the inhabitants – Miners if ever they were any:

In a secret place lies a cave of gold
So deep and dark it makes your blood run cold.

In the cave of gold lives a race of men
Who will never see the sun again.

They are pale as slugs and blind as moles,
In place of eyes they have little red coals.

In place of hearts they have blocks of ice,
And they dine each day off the tails of mice.

But better than mice they like Fanish flesh,
Especially when it is young and fresh.

Yes, Fanish flesh is their favourite dish,
And when they catch you they go like this:

Gobble, gobble, gobble . . .

And at this point the rope would be turned faster and faster until the contender could no longer keep pace, and the winner would be the one who held out longest, to the highest count of 'gobbles'.

These rumours of hidden riches to be had for the seeking could scarcely have come at a worse moment. Eaglet, small and skew though he was, had at least been a Fane and male to our credit; now that he was taken from us, my faction was indeed, to use the Regent's expression, cut down to just a handful of women and furry-wurries. (Not all of us silly, maybe, but it made little difference number-wise.) Dola was rising thirteen: in a year's time, or even sooner if she took a husband, she would be able to govern on her own account. I was still in name Alexa, Princess Regent, Ruler of All the Fanes, but it was clear as day to everyone, even to the blind head-stableman at his scrubbing bucket in the kitchen, that my power was slipping, and slipping fast.

At the next sitting of Council, like a threatened piece on the chequerboard, back-stepping to avoid being toppled, I finally gave in and granted the fundamental change of tactics that everyone had been clamouring for for so long: no longer defence, but attack. I hesitated as long as I dared before doing so, but the air in the room was so thick with impatience and ill will, and the faces confronting me so set and hostile, that if I hadn't, I think the first attack might have taken place there and then, against me. (Which would have helped no one, or so I reasoned quickly: neither me, nor the Fanes, nor the Miners and their allies, nor anyone at all.) When I donned the head-dress to make my final pronouncement, I heard, quite distinctly through all the fur, the Commander mutter, 'Darned nanny-goat, I hope it smothers her!' With real venom in his voice. And I am not quite sure, but I think I saw the Regent, with a nasty sparkly look in his eye, reach for the hilt of his dagger and then let go of it again in disappointment when I opened my mouth to give consent.

Muley congratulated me afterwards on what he said was a very wise decision. He had a medal in his hand which he showed me. 'Look, Highness,' he said, 'on one side is the head of a man, and on the other,' and he flipped the medal over, 'is the body of a she-wolf suckling her cubs. Would you say they are pictures of the same thing? Of course you wouldn't. And yet it is still the same medal, is it not? Two different faces, but only the one medal. Well, try to think of today's decision in the same way. Attack may look different from defence, but if it is carried out for the right reasons, namely to bring the war to an end, then it isn't really different at all. It is just defence's other face, so to speak.'

There was something not quite right about this reasoning, but I didn't have a medallion of my own handy, so I couldn't really work out what it was. All I could think of saying, and this not until later that night when I was discussing the matter with Lois, was that if attack was just the other face of defence then it was an even uglier one. With which Lois all too grimly agreed.

'You know what the next step will be, Alexa, don't you?' he said, taking a lock of my hair and holding it close to the flame of the candle so that it glinted. 'This. The gold. The Miners' gold that everyone's talking about. That'll be the next thing they're after, or I'm a beaver.'

'You very nearly are a beaver. And my hair doesn't look like gold any more, it's losing colour.'

He ignored this, he was in too serious a mood. 'They won't put it like that, mind you, not in so many words. No doubt old Craftyribs will pull another of his tricks to try and prove to you that it's right and just and the best way of putting an end to the fighting. But that's what he and the Regent will be wanting from you next: permission to start a treasure hunt. And then, when they find the treasure, permission to steal it, and permission to keep it. "We need the gold to buy peace from our neighbours," they will say. "Without their riches the Miners will find no one to do their fighting for them and the war will fizzle out as a result." But you don't buy peace with stolen gold, Alexa, you buy submission. And with submission comes more hatred and more fear – and loads more trouble.'

It seemed to me that with this typical Salvan forecast Lois was being unnecessarily gloomy and rather unfair. I didn't like it when he called Muley names, not even Craftyribs which was one of the politer ones. (And I knew Muley was against the idea of treasure hunting anyway, because when I'd asked his opinion about Aurona he had shaken his head and said you should never waste time looking for anything hidden; only fools did that, clever people first made sure where to look.) 'Why do you always lump Muley and the Regent together like that?' I asked. 'Muley isn't on anyone's side in particular, he just tries to be helpful and smooth things out.'

Lois grunted and murmured something uncomplimentary about smoothness being Muley's stock-in-trade.

I didn't want us to argue so I pretended I hadn't heard. 'Besides,' I went on, trying to sound more convinced than perhaps I was, 'the Fanes have never been plunderers. This business of Aurona – it's only talk, only gossip. The place may not exist for all we know, and even if it does exist and the Regent manages to find it, no right-thinking Fane is going to turn thief and follow him there, just because His Grossness tells them to.'

'You really think so, Alexa? What if the order comes from Dolasilla? What then?'

This was a horrible thought and I was almost angry at Lois for thinking it. I shook my head, hard, so that the lock of hair jerked out of his grasp. 'No,' I said, 'never. Dola will never turn plunderer either. She's my daughter, she's *our* daughter, she would never do a thing like that. She's tough, hot-headed, maybe even ruthless at times, but there's no greed in her heart, of that I'm sure.'

There was a slight movement under the bed-clothes where my feet were: it was Lois crossing his toes. 'Let's hope you're right about that, my love,' he murmured. 'You know what I think about metal and what it does to people – well, Dolasilla has been very close to a large amount of it now for a very long time. Let's hope her heart can stand the test.'

I hoped so too. Oh, goodness, how hard I hoped it.

CHAPTER FOURTEEN

Poppies

For a while it looked as if Lois's worst fears had come true: Dolasilla took to the warpath like a duckling to pond-water or a wolfcub to the woods, and the Commander and his troops followed her in a pack, cheering and triumphant, wherever she led. The stronghold of the Latrones, the rock of the Peleghetes, Dark Castle where the Lastojeres had their home – all these places fell, almost unresisting and in the space of a season, to Fane attacks. I had said my kinsfolk were not plunderers, and I don't think they were, not really, not yet, but each time the assault party returned home their saddles would be laden with gifts of surrender from the vanquished tribes, which if not plunder were dangerously close to it. Fànes had never been so thriving and busy, the

Fanes themselves had never been so bumptious and full of beans. The war, carried on now in other folks' territories, out of sight and hearing, not to mention smell, had become a game to them – a marvellous game, with prizes every time. They would gather in the courtyard and watch, smiles all over their faces, as the Regent waddled out to embrace his darling warrior-daughter, back from yet another easy victory, and run his fingers, merchant-like, over the spoils. 'Jewels,' he would announce, holding them up for an instant for everyone to see, and then stashing them away quickly in a special wheeled chest with the Crow Mount emblem on it, scratched out but still visible. 'Two copper rings, two copper bracelets, one *gold* brooch. Yum, yum, yum, wonder where they got that from? Plates. Goblets. Shaving tackle – Oho, I fear the King of the Latrones will have to grow a beard now that he's lost his razor. Three salt-cellars. Empty. Pity. Four *very* fetching spoons . . .'

I took no part in these gatherings, but looked on from a distance, misgivings piling up inside me faster than the trophies in the chest. More and more metal, more and more celebrations, less and less talk of peace. What was happening to my Fanish kinsmen? What was happening to Lois's and my daughter? (Or was she not Lois's daughter after all but the Regent's – in name and in character? That would explain a lot.) What would become of us when she held in her own two hands, not only the reins of her poor little battle-weary ponies, but the reins of government? Where would she lead us? What other conquests would she want our soldiers to undertake? Would she never tire of charging round the place with the Raietta on her forehead, shouting, 'Follow me! Follow me! Fànes or death!', playing the Warrior Queen?

The answer to these questions, and to the last in particular, came in the most unexpected way; and although it was a sad way and led to all sorts of terrible consequences, I couldn't help being happy about it in a corner of my heart as well as sad, because of all answers it was the one I most wanted to hear. Indeed, in a very small corner, I still am happy. Despite everything.

(My young listeners of today have difficulty understanding this. 'But that means,' they say, puzzled, 'you were happy about the Prince's death?' No, I tell them, not his death: I was sad about his death. I was happy about what his death told me; it is different. But this tends to puzzle them even more, because to them, who are very practical-minded, the episode merely proves that Dola was a crack markswoman and the Prince himself rather foolish not to have remembered this. 'Dead men don't speak,' they object, 'so his death can't have told you anything. And you can't be happy and sad at the same time, neither, 'less you're barmy.' So at this point, instead of trying to explain that, yes they do, and yes you can, you can be happy and almost anything in my experience, except happy and ashamed, I usually go straight ahead with the story and trust that they will understand when they are older.)

What happened was this. On a cold bright day of autumn when the nip of snow-to-come was already in the air, Dola set out with her chosen band of soldiers for the Fortress of Cadubren: the Cadubrenes being the only enemy tribe, apart from the still fierce and defiant Cajutes, that had not, as Muley called it in his usual polite fashion, been 'dealt with'. The Commander accompanied her as second-in-charge, his Deputy went along as third, and Ey de Net, who always volunteered for this post when he had no Eaglet to look after, tacked on behind as Dola's shield-bearer. The Regent stayed at home, being simply too fat and too scared for this kind of outing.

I, for this once, rode with the fighters. I'm still not quite sure why. Partly to keep an eye on Dola, I suppose, and partly because it seemed cowardly of me not to, when I was the one who had ordered this series of attacks, or at any rate allowed it to take place. 'Always take your responsibilities on your own pair of shoulders and look them straight in the face,' my father used to tell me; and apart from the neck-twisting involved I knew that he was right: it was my duty to know what 'dealing with' consisted in, not just in words but on the ground and in the flesh. Perhaps I also thought, just by being there when the attack took place, I could stop things getting out of hand. Or perhaps I even thought I could stop things altogether.

Dola, knowing nothing of these reasons, was thrilled to pieces to have me with her. She came into my room well before sunrise, almost catching Lois off his guard but not quite, and insisted on our dressing for battle together, exactly as if we were just any mother and daughter dolling themselves up for a feast-day. 'What shall I wear, Alexa? What are *you* going to wear? Something light, I think, don't you: we've got a lot of riding to do first. Shall I leave my head bare so that the soldiers can see the Raietta in my hair? Or shall I wear a helmet and try and fix the Raietta on the front?' (Oh, that dratted stone, how I had come to hate it.) 'Sonia,' – Sonia had meanwhile appeared in the doorway, sent for by Lois – 'Sonia, you wouldn't be a treasure, would you, and go and see if you can't find some good strong twine to tie my crown on?' Never since her childhood had I seen Dola so friendly and chatty in my company; never, although I tried not to let this show, had I felt myself more at a loss in hers.

Her high spirits infected the rest of the party like Schniappa (maybe the Shaman had been doling out some of that too, he usually did before a battle), and when the soldiers set forth, had you not known the real nature of their business, you would have thought them just a group of overgrown children off on some harmless jaunt. They laughed, sang, chattered, and the sun glinted on their teeth and in the whites of their smiling eyes and on the points of their shining weapons, and every so often, to guffaws of merriment, one of them would pick up a horn and blow rude noises on it. Prrrp! Prrrp! Prrrp!

'Work up an appetite, girls and boys!' Nurse called out to them from the battlements in her daft fashion. 'Come back with roses in your cheeks!'

'Yar, yar! Roses! And poppies too!' they shouted back. It struck me afterwards as strange they should have used this word, 'poppies', but I suppose it was only because they are red.

We reached the Cadubrenes' stronghold in mid-morning, when everyone inside was busy eating. The Commander rubbed his hands together and said it was the perfect moment for an attack, since there was nothing better than catching the enemy with their bibs on in place of breastplates, unless it was catching them with the trots. But I managed to persuade him to wait until we had given fair warning: it was the only rule left that neither side had yet broken, and I didn't want us to be the first. Dola, I was glad to see, agreed with me.

'The Princess Regent is right, Commander,' she said quietly: she never seemed to have to raise her voice to make herself heard, not even at times like these. 'We are not marauders, we are warriors. We will send the Cadubrenes a proper challenge, explaining exactly what we intend to do and why, and give them time to answer it as they see fit. You never know, they may come out with a white duster in their hands and the keys of the castle on a cushion, the way the Lastojeres did. I hope not because it's probably our last chance this year to get some decent action, but we ought at least to give them a chance to do so if they wish.' And, calm and unruffled as a puddle with ice on it, she dismounted, unhitched her travelling pack from her saddle, drew from it a small slate and a piece of chalk, and sat down and began writing out a message.

Now, I say I don't believe in blaming things on Fate, and no more I do. (Only a very lazy person like Zeno would allow his life to be shaped for him by a trio of blind old fumbly women with a weaving kit, the way he taught me in his lessons.) But for what happened next it is hard to see who else was responsible. True, the written message was unusual – nobody normally brought writing equipment into the fray, let alone used it – but as Dola said afterwards, a hatchet thrown into the wood of the drawbridge only says one thing, 'Attack!', whereas she wanted to say several. True, it was also unusual to deliver the message by hand, as Ey de Net now did, carrying it right up to the back gateway and placing it gently in the trading-basket, instead of shooting it over the walls attached to an arrow; but there was no forethought in this, no will to deceive, it was just that you can't very well shoot a slate into the air without breaking it. Besides, apart from the brief meeting with their court tutor all those many years ago (which I didn't remember anyway until after-wards when it was too late), how were we to know that neither the Prince of Cadubren nor any of his people could read? And, when Dola and I couldn't even guess each other's, how were we to know the secrets of the poor young man's silly, vain and just as badly-tutored heart?

He thought Dola was in love with him, you see. He had apparently thought this for a very long time, ever since she had downed her bow on him once in the course of a battle and refrained from shooting, thus sparing his life. The incident must have been due to chance – when we were told about it Dola couldn't even remember it happen-ing, although she said she did have to interrupt her shooting once on account of a bee in her eye. But the Prince thought she had spared him on purpose, out of love for him, and from that day forth he had begun to return this imaginary passion and to cherish dreams of marrying her.

Such are the perils, so I tell my young and not always diligent audience, of an incomplete educa-tion. The Prince thought that Dola was in love with him, and that on the slate she had written him a love letter, and that with her armed guard (champing one and all to be at his throat, had he only stopped to take a closer look) she was now waiting outside his gate for him to fly to her and clasp her in his arms.

So he rode quickly – another little twist of Fate's thread. I can see it all as if it were still happening, so often have I been through it in my mind, both deliberately and not: the drawbridge flapping open in an arc and bouncing on the hard, sun-baked ground; the horses' hooves thundering over it and battening it down as the Prince and his attendants gallop forth in a rush. Then the dust and the glare and the difficulty of picking out figures in the group, outlined as it is by the sudden light in the archway behind. I can sense the fidgeting of our own horses, and the closing of our ranks when it becomes clear that the enemy soldiers are making straight towards us. I see Ey de Net, shading his forehead with his hand and peering into the cloud of dust with those incredible eyes of his, and shouting, 'Wait! The front one's got something! He's waving something! Wait! I can't see what it is!' And I can feel, or better, smell the fear of our soldiers, turning now to panic as still no order is given. 'Holy Deer!' they shriek. 'Wassit? Wassit? Make up your mind, they'll be on us in a blink!'

Then, menacing like the puff of a snake, I hear close by me the tautening of Dola's bowstring: Ziiiih! 'Say when,' she instructs Ey de Net calmly, as if they were carrying out the filling of a mug or the heaping of a plate, or some other everyday task,

'I don't want to muff it.' Then, louder, to the others, 'Ready, everyone? Draw now, and release one count after me.' And, still in that matter-of-fact, conversational voice she begins to count: 'One . . . Two . . . Three . . .'

Ey de Net is far more agitated: it is no joke to face an onslaught like this armed with a shield that is meant for someone else. 'Wait!' he repeats in a high-pitched voice, as the hooves thunder nearer and nearer. 'I see it now. It's a rag, a duster. A sign.'

'White?' asks Dola, fitting it in between her counting: Four . . . White? . . . Five . . . Her steadiness is amazing, I can see why her soldiers trust her every move. 'Is it a white duster?'

'No. Red!' squeaks Ey de Net. 'Red, red, red! Red for war!'

He is right, of course, about the colour, but not about the duster. Dola draws a deep breath, stands still as a rock for an instant, and on the count of six, without any more questions or waiting (and even I, I may tell you, am beginning to think it's about time), opens her hand to release the string. 'War be it then!' she whispers in the arrow's wake, and then in a huge voice which you wouldn't think possible could come from so slender a throat, 'Arrrgh! Seven! Let 'em fly!'

At this point in a battle, no matter what the enemy does, whether it falters and you lunge at it, or continues its charge and you lock, there is usually an ear-splitting and mind-baffling noise.

What Dola called the Warrior's Thrill, and what I call the Warrior's Fog because I can see nothing thrilling about it at all, takes over, and all is crashing and neighing and shouting and muddle. You feel no fear, no worry, no pity, because you do not feel: like Eaglet's bear you become a doll in the hands of the War God, and you only hope your stuffing will remain inside.

After Dola's order, therefore, I braced myself for the impact and drew my sword and patted my pony's neck with the flat of it to keep her calm: a frightened mount can be more dangerous than the enemy. I wished fleetingly I had put side-flaps on her bridle to keep her head straight, but it was so long since I had taken part in an open encounter that I'd forgotten. Out of the corner of my eye I saw Lois doing something to his nails: chewing them, I think, to sharpen them – they and his teeth were still the only weapons he allowed himself to use.

I braced myself and so did we all, but nothing happened. No clash came. The cloud of dust that none but Ey de Net's sight could penetrate came to a fuzzy halt some twenty paces in front of us, and before we could surge to the attack Ey de Net himself leaped forward from our midst with Dola's heavy shield held crosswise in his hands to block our advance. If Dola hadn't trained her pony so well I think it might have trampled him. 'No!' he screamed, in the same high-pitched tone as before:

his voice, which was broken when he came to us, seemed to have reverted to a child's. 'Back! Hold back, for the Sun God's sake! They're unarmed! They've got no weapons! Get back! Get back!'

How he managed to restrain us at this late moment, I don't know, but he did. Sawing and jostling we reined in our mounts and slumped back in our saddles with our weapons trailing from our hands, and watched, mystified, as the dust began to settle round the company of Cadubren riders, and their figures began to emerge.

By now I have practically explained what happened, so I don't think I need go over the details of what the Prince looked like, lying there on the ground with Dola's arrow-shaft sticking out of his forehead and a bunch of wilted poppies in his hand and an expression of utter surprise on his poor lovesick face. Nor need I say what his companions looked like, or what they said to us, or how they cried and shook their fists and tore the poppies from their leader's hands and threw them in Dola's direction: 'Cursed! Cursed! Cursed! The Gods curse you for ever, cruel Queen of the Fanes!' But I must describe the effect it had on Dola, because this was her turning point; in a sense, her moment of healing.

It was strange, when she was cleverer than all of us put together, but it seemed to take her longer than anyone else to understand what had happened. For what seemed ages she just sat there on her pony, letting the rain of spits and threats and insults from the Prince's companions pour over her unnoticed: you couldn't tell what she was thinking, or even if she was thinking at all. Then, with a shake of her head which dislodged the Raietta crown and sent it clattering onto the ground where Ey de Net retrieved it, she slithered off her pony and walked slowly over to where the body of the Prince was lying, parting the ring of hostile Cadubrenes as if by magic or sheer force of will.

They watched her like hawks for a false move, and I them, but she walked like a dream-walker, and I think they were afraid to touch her. She stood there a moment, beside the body, staring hard, taking it all in. Then she dropped gently to her knees and, to a chorus of shock and disapproval from the Prince's escort, who still didn't move to stop her, traced a line with her finger from the young man's punctured forehead to his heart.

I didn't hear what she said, I wasn't close enough, but I saw her lips move, and noticed the Cadubren soldier standing next to her reach out and put a restraining hand on his neighbour's arm and whisper something. Her words, whatever they were, seemed to be quenching their anger.

When she had finished speaking she got to her feet, and in a hush that had now become total silence, save for the blowing of the horses' nostrils and the jingling of their bits, she reached into her quiver and drew forth an arrow, which she snapped in two over her knee, Toc! like a piece of kindling wood. Then another, then another, until the quiver was empty. 'Witness, Cadubrenes,' she said as she did so, still not loudly, but loud enough for us all to hear. 'Witness, Fanes. I have done a great wrong today: I have killed a man who rode towards me in friendship, armed with nothing but a bunch of flowers. If you who are his friends wish to take my life in return, you may do so, and put an end to my shame; I will offer no resistance, and neither will my troops, I vouch for this. But whether you do or whether you don't, here and now – in front of you all, so there is no going back – I make this vow: Never again will I bear arms, never again will I lead my troops to battle, never again will I kill a fellow human, friend or foe though he or she may be. I swear it by the Bear God of the Underworld, and may he take me to his cave and keep me there if ever I break my pledge.'

Dola was at her best, of course, when making solemn speeches in front of an audience, but this time I knew she wasn't playing for effect: she was saying what she meant because she meant it. This horrible accident had opened her eyes for her, shown her something that I had been yearning for her to see all along, namely the wicked, gormless wastefulness of war. She even looked different – smaller, nicer, less of a Queen and more of the twelve-year-old girl that she was.

I wanted to go to her and hug her and tell her

how proud I was she had come to her senses at last, but the situation was still delicate, and I thought it wiser to stay put. Both sides – the Fanes as well as the Cadubrenes – seemed nonplussed by her announcement, almost stunned, and for a long stretched-out moment during which time itself appeared to dither, no one moved or said anything at all. Had they heard her aright? Was Queen Dolasilla of the shining Raietta really renouncing warfare? And if she was, where did that leave them? How were they to take it? What were they to do?

Dola told me afterwards she had acted on impulse, but like it is with all good leaders, the impulse she acted on was correct. If she had made any other move the Cadubrenes would probably not have forgiven her the way they did; if she had made the same move at any other time the Fanes would not have forgiven her either. As it was, just by being sincere, she gained the respect of followers and foe alike. I'm not sure who did so first, whether it was me, or the Commander, or Ey de Net, or even one of the soldiers, but slowly, one by one, the members of our group began surrendering their weapons. (Arrows only, of course: we all knew, even I, that it was the gesture that counted.) Some, taking Dola's example, broke them over their knees first, others simply laid them on the ground at the feet of the fallen Prince, like a farewell gift or a consolation prize. Soon there was a pile as high as a man's kneecap.

Without Lois, however, I don't know whether this gesture would have been enough. The Cadubrenes were moved but their mood was still doubtful: you could see their eyes shifting from arrows to Prince to arrows again, and their expressions hardening and softening by turns as they tried to make up their minds. Trust or mistrust? Forgiveness or revenge? You could also see them – one or two of them anyway – glancing back at the fortress with narrowed eyes, as if measuring the distance and the time it would take for their troops to reach us, once alerted. Which way their mood would finally have swung is impossible to say, they probably didn't even know themselves, but at this crucial moment, *before* the swing, while the two options hung even, like a pair of well-matched piglets on a balance, and our futures with them, Lois strolled quietly over to the arrow-pile where everyone had cast their weapons, and without the slightest hesitation or indication of what he was about to do, put his hand to his mouth and with a sudden wrench tore the nail from the forefinger of his right hand by the roots and spat it on the heap along with the arrows. (From which place I later retrieved it when no one was looking: I couldn't bear to leave it there.) 'My token,' he said, but his voice came out so altered by pain that he had to repeat it. 'My peace token. Please accept it, I have no other weapon to offer.'

It was so swiftly and simply done that it was some moments before any of us, even me, were aware of exactly what had happened. When the Cadubrenes realized, however, their attitude towards us changed immediately: it was indeed the tipping of the scales. The young man who had earlier been held back by his neighbour, and who I judged was probably the Prince's closest friend, perhaps even his brother, stepped forward and with great gentleness, careful to avoid touching the lacerated finger, took Lois's hand in his own and shook it in sign of agreement. No words and no fuss, but it was the peace accord we had all been hoping for. 'Don't just stand there gaping,' he ordered his companions, who were doing just that. 'Find a bit of cloth, bind it up for him. Can't you see he's losing blood?' Then he turned to Lois and relaxed his mouth so that he almost smiled. 'Strong teeth you have, Salvan,' he said. 'Strong will too. Was it difficult? Do you think I could do the same?'

I was relieved to see that Lois's colour was coming back already: after the wrench he had gone like clay. 'I doubt it,' he answered. 'Your nails are different – softer; they'd break first.'

'Ah,' the young man said. 'My nails. Not my resolve?' And then, when Lois shrugged in reply and looked vaguely embarrassed, he really did smile.

After this, my memories of that ill-starred yet in some ways oh, so fortunate morning become a little vague. Probably because the Cadubrenes, to seal the new pact between us, and to send off their poor Prince in style and drown their sorrows and wash away the rancours the way custom requires, now took us back to the fortress and offered us an incredible amount to drink, which we were unable to refuse. I remember, after the handshake, everyone suddenly talking together in a rush – questioning, apologizing, explaining, and then apologizing again; creating a kind of contest of courtesies which, had the matter not been so tragic and we not so closely involved in it, might really have sounded quite funny. '*We* shouldn't have let him take the poppies, only they were the only flowers to hand, and he did so want to offer flowers.' 'No, no, *we* should have waited until we saw what they were: we were too hasty, too mistrusting.' '*We* shouldn't have hired that cheating tutor, we knew there was something fishy about him.' 'Hardly your fault, we nearly hired him ourselves. It is *us* who should have remembered and made allowances.'

I remember gabbling away in the same fashion myself, all the time trying to hide the happiness which was welling up inside me fast, and which I knew was dreadfully out of place. Dola was mine again, I could recognize her as my daughter and be proud of her. Her heart, which Lois had been so worried about, was safe, whole, unblistered, and that was all that mattered.

In the fumes of the drinking bout she threw her

arms round me and we clung to each other like a she-bear and cub, making our own private peace in the midst of the general one: we didn't need to say anything – words could come later – we just understood by touch. She hugged Lois too and made him sit with us while she rewound his finger dressing, which moved me even more than our own reunion, if this were possible, because it felt – just for a moment anyway – that the three of us belonged together, like a family. And a little later on – although things were getting very blurred in my mind by then, so that it might in fact have been quite a lot later on – she asked him, seeing he was so good at dislodging things, to take her crown from Ey de Net and prise the Raietta from its setting for her, because she no longer wanted to wear this symbol of her former military power.

'I will have a red stone set in its place,' she announced to those of the assembly who were still sober enough to listen. 'Red, to remind me of your Prince's blood I shed so wrongly, and the poppies that were his last gift to me. Red, too, to remind me of my shame.'

Attention was scant, but the applause was deafening, and the bowl of Schniappa, which the Cadubrenes called Life Liquor, was passed round yet again, and the tears of sadness and drunkenness and mirth and relief and companionship and I know not what else, flowed even faster and spilled and mingled until no one, not even Lois who had drunk less than anyone on account of not feeling up to it, could distinguish which were which.

Only when, almost in darkness, we crawled into our saddles again and began the journey home, did my head clear enough for me to wonder what the Regent's reaction would be to this new and unforeseen development: the changed Dolasilla, the broken arrows, the discarded Raietta, and the empty crown waiting for its blood-red stone.

Ah, yes, I was forgetting, and a new son-in-law too. Because on our way back Dola confided to me that she and Ey de Net were secretly promised to one another and intended to get married as soon as possible: she would announce the fact to the Regent tonight, along with everything else. (And I was not to gasp like that either, she added – with a laugh, to take the sting away – because after Lois I was hardly in a position to say who she should or who she shouldn't fall in love with, was I now?)

CHAPTER FIFTEEN

Noises in the Night

I knew danger was hovering over us now. I didn't even need to use my nose, I could see it, feel it, almost taste it in the food that night at supper, as I watched the Regent trying to digest the news of the day's happenings along with his soup and failing uglily with both. But although he swelled tighter than a toad, and roared and fumed and threatened, and hurled terrible oaths like GODS' GUTS!!! and ROT THE HOLY OAK!!! and PEACE BE BLUBBERED!!! and hurled the crockery too, and swore that he would see to all our funerals before consenting to Dola's marriage with a CONNIVING, BASE-BLOODED, WEASEL-FATHERED RUNT like Ey de Net, I still didn't realize quite how close the danger was or how big.

Late into the night – so late that Lois didn't dare join me but remained on guard outside in his sheepskin – I heard noises coming from the Regent's quarters. Voices, thumpings, clashings, comings and goings; what sounded like heavy objects being dragged across the floor. I imagined he was venting his rage on the furniture or the cooking pots: there was precious else left in the way of breakables now he had gone through the tableware. But here too reality outstripped me and I imagined wrong.

In a lull between noises, and just as I was thinking of paying another visit to the tower-room, where I had sent Dola and Eaglet and Ey de Net to spend the night, under the watchful eye of the Commander and the pick of our armed guards (I hadn't realized the full extent of our danger, maybe, but I wasn't taking any chances, not on *that* score; I had even locked away the dogs), I heard a knock on the door.

It was Muley. Or to be more precise, it was Lois, teeth bared and hackles raised like pine needles, with Muley standing behind him, waiting for admittance.

He looked extremely nervous. Muley, I mean. Lois, what with pain and vigilance and blood-stained bandage, was not a very cosy figure to be accosted by in the darkness.

'Shall I let him in?' Lois asked, his voice closer to a growl than I had ever heard it.

'Of course,' I said sharply to make up for his

rudeness, opening wide the door and beckoning. Even in unusual circumstances like these, Muley's presence seemed to invite calm, serenity, and I was glad he had risked the trip: it wasn't everyone who dared venture forth during one of the Regent's tantrums.

'Want me to stay?'

'No, Lois, you know that won't be necessary.'

'I *hope* it won't be necessary,' Lois corrected me. And then, quietly, in Salvan, 'Better not be, or I'll rip his scrawny throat with the nails I've got left.'

Muley flinched before stepping inside, and nearly dropped the candle he was holding, so I have the impression he understood the language. I wouldn't be surprised; I wouldn't be surprised about anything regarding Muley any more.

'Your . . . er . . . your . . . er . . . faithful bodyguard doesn't much like me, Highness, I'm afraid,' he said when I had closed the door and we were alone.

I thought there was a trace of irony, almost of insolence, in the way he hesitated after the 'your', as if what he had wanted to say was 'your lover' or 'your bedfellow', but I paid no heed. People often talk in a funny way when they are jumpy.

'And *I* don't much like *him* when he is so surly,' I replied. 'But we're all on edge tonight, and you must forgive him. What did you want to see me about? Have you seen the Regent? Have you any idea what he's up to?'

Muley sat down on the bed – without being invited, which again struck me as slightly out of character in one so good mannered – and began tapping the toes of his shoes together. If he hadn't come of his own accord I'd have thought he was impatient to be elsewhere. 'I have *heard* the Regent, Highness,' he said, 'and I have an idea he is up to mischief.'

My own idea exactly, although it worried me to hear it said. 'What sort of mischief?' I asked.

Muley kept his eyes carefully on his bobbing shoe-points and sighed. 'That is not for me to say,' he replied. 'The man is very hot tempered, and he has reason to be tonight; he might do a lot of things. Things that he will regret, no doubt, when he has simmered down and Queen Dolasilla has come back to her senses, but in the meantime he'll have done them and no one will be able to undo them.'

I had no hackles like Lois, but I could feel the place where they would have been if I did, tingling. Out of fear or some other emotion, I couldn't tell. 'He can't harm Dolasilla,' I said, far louder than I intended. 'The Fanes wouldn't allow it. And what do you mean, Come back to her senses? The way I see it, she's only just come *into* her senses.'

'Of course,' Muley said promptly. 'Of course. And that is the way I see it too; I was merely speaking from the Regent's point of view. But . . .'

and here he hestitated and poured a little candle grease into the palm of his hand and began stirring it with his finger, 'are we to take it that the change is permanent? That she will really and truly never bear arms again?'

What a thing to ask, when a vow has been made. I was quite shocked. 'How else are we to take it?' I said indignantly. 'You aren't suggesting Dolasilla is one to go back on her word, are you? If so, you haven't understood the first thing about her. She is *good*, Muley. Believe me, under the bluster she is good and generous and true. I know that now, and I think deep down I've always known it, only I never really had proof of it until today. Remember what you said to me once about my having no rennet in my heart? Well, today, with the Prince's death, the rennet has drained out of Dolasilla's heart too. And, unless I'm very much mistaken, it's never coming back. The wars are over, Muley. Not in the way we would have chosen, perhaps, but our wishes have been granted, and we are in for a long and much needed spell of peace.'

This was quite a speech for me, but Muley seemed to have listened to it very attentively. His foot-tapping had stopped, and his finger was poised over the spilt wax, in which, now that it had hardened, I could see he had drawn a cross. 'I don't think you're mistaken at all, Highness,' he said thoughtfully after a long pause, during which his fidgeting started up again, faster than before.

'Mothers usually sense these things better than anyone. Which is why I have come to you. I wanted to make sure, you see; it is always my policy to make sure.'

I could find nothing to argue with in that. 'Perhaps you should speak to Dolasilla herself, then,' I suggested. 'Just to be on the safe side.'

I said Muley couldn't surprise me any more, and it's true, he can't, but he surprised me now by bursting out laughing. 'The safe side, Highness!' he chortled, jiggling up and down and splattering a fresh flow of candle grease all over the bed. 'Oh, that's a good one! The safe side! Excuse me, but your Highness has such a funny way of putting things sometimes. Yes, indeed, the safe side – or the right side – isn't that where all of us want to be?'

I was beginning by now to find his behaviour really weird, and I think he must have realized this because he snuffed his amusement immediately, like you snuff a flame. 'I would have spoken to Queen Dolasilla,' he went on, in a completely serious, almost *too*-serious-to-be-serious manner, 'but she is rather – what shall we call it? – rather inaccessible this evening. The guards wouldn't open the door.'

So he had tried to see Dola. Well, I supposed there was nothing wrong in that. (Although there *was*. Oh, gods and goddesses, there was! It makes my flesh crawl, even now, to think what evil he might have done to her that night if he had succeeded in getting past the guards.) 'You can speak to her tomorrow,' I told him, 'when things have calmed down a little.'

I thought I saw his amusement surface again, but if so he was quick to hide it. 'Tomorrow,' he said softly, almost dreamily, 'tomorrow. Tomorrow is the day that never breaks, Highness, did you know that? Time flows, and we bob along on its current, but the current only washes us through the banks of a tonight and a today, a here and a now. There are so many things I would prefer to do tomorrow, but alas, if I am to *do* them, and not just think about them or talk about them, it can only be tonight.' And with this he gave another little flurry of taps, then put his feet squarely on the floor and prepared to rise.

After he had gone, which he did soon afterwards without answering my question about the Regent or indeed saying anything useful at all, I was left wondering about the reason for this strange late-night visit. And to some extent (when I can bear to think of Muley, which isn't often) I wonder still. Was it really indecision about which side to choose, the way his words seemed to indicate? Possible but unlikely: from the care and patience he had put into his plans I think he must have made up his mind – *and* his baggage – already, the very moment we got back to the castle with our news. Was it curiosity, then? Or spite? Or a desire to gloat at me in my plight while I was still unaware of it? I shall never know. I have a suspicion, though, that the real reason, more sinister than all the others put together when you come to think about it, was simply that he was unable, for politeness' sake, to leave without saying goodbye.

Next morning, anyway, he was gone from Fànes without leaving a trace, and so was the Regent with the treasure chest on wheels, and so were several of our Fanish soldiers – the greediest, the least faithful, the easiest to lure away. And so were many of our horses and many of our carts and much of our hay besides. And – a bitterer blow still, and one that sent howls of anger and dismay round the castle when the loss was discovered – so were *all* our new blond-iron weapons from the Armoury. Even Eaglet's special suit, too small to fit anyone but him, was missing from its stand. Overnight and without any of us noticing it, we had been deceived and disarmed and deserted.

CHAPTER SIXTEEN

Theft and Treachery

The Regent's treachery was the first of that day's surprises but it was not the worst, not by a long mark. The worst surprise was still in store; waiting, like the wolves do, for evening-time to make its spring. And as yet it was still morning.

After I had broken the news to Dola and Eaglet (which I tried to do gently because, after all, being his children, or sort of, their feelings for the Regent were more complicated than mine), I called a meeting of Council to examine the situation and decide what must be done.

It was a disorderly meeting because our thoughts were disorderly, mine most of all. Everyone kept shouting, 'Treason!' and, 'Traitors!' and, 'Thieves!' and asking questions all at once which nobody could answer. Or not yet. Where had Muley and the Regent gone? What time had they left? Could we still catch up with them and try to recover some of our stuff? Why had they ratted on us like that? Had anybody heard them? If so, why for holy holly's sake had no one tried to stop them? What did they want, anyway, with so many weapons? Who did they plan to use them against? And what were we to do now with so few? Could our smiths forge more? Did we have the metal? Did we have the know-how, or had Master Turncoat Mule-bones carried off the secret in his skull of a head? Some of the questions were not questions at all but just plain wails: What was to become of us? Why were the gods so angry? Why was our star, that had been so bright, now riding so low? Ah, the Raietta, our lucky white Raietta, Queen Dolasilla should never have plucked it from its rightful place in her crown!

Zeno always used to say that it makes for clarity to put things in words. I think he meant writing them down *before* you say them, but anyway, after I had finished answering all these questions, or trying to, I was indeed a bit clearer in my mind. The Regent almost certainly had gone to Crow Mount – there was nowhere else for him to go. He had gone there because he was a trouble-maker and a grasper, and he wanted to go on making trouble and grasping on an ever bigger scale. Maybe the plan for flight was in his head already, maybe not, maybe Muley had put it there, maybe it just grew, but the events of yesterday had evidently made up his mind for him: he would go back to his craggy roost, armed to the teeth, and carry on his plundering from there, unhindered by 'soppies' and 'spoilsports' and 'badger-lovers' and whatever else he called us.

Plundering what, though, and from whom? That was the most urgent question to find an answer to. How deep did the man's treachery go, and how big was his greed? Even though he had taken with him all he could cart, Fànes was still brimming with riches. Would he turn against us – against his own blood, his own daughter, who until yesterday had been the pride of his life, or so he had always said – in order to get them? Or was Lois right and was his real aim the fabled gold hoard of Aurona?

At the meeting I plumped for Aurona, because I didn't want people worrying unnecessarily, but in my heart I was not so sure. After all, if the Regent was really as greedy as I feared, he might want both: the Miners' gold *and* the wealth of Fànes. And as for turning against Dola – well, when I thought back on his furious purple face of the previous evening, and the threats he'd uttered, and the way smoke had come out of his ears, or almost, when Dola had told him about her engagement to Ey de Net, I reckoned he'd already turned. And at that very instant. It is a serious accusation to bring against anyone, I know, because fathers of any sort are not supposed to feel that way about their daughters and there's the rope for those that do, but I honestly think that on top of everying else the man was jealous of Dolasilla, like a spurned lover.

With regard to weapons, our position was not good. The master smith spoke after me and confirmed everyone's worst fears: we had a fair amount of raw metal left – the traitors had not been able to take it all, although from the mess they had made of the smithy it looked as if they'd tried – but the secret of the blond iron was, alas, lost and gone, perhaps for ever. Mulebones had never allowed anyone to be present during the final stage of the layering, always insisted on doing it himself, even the heating and the stoking of the furnace, and now we knew why. We could try to work out the technique for ourselves maybe, but it would take luck and it would take time, and – not to sound gloomy, but we seemed to be running out of both.

'The secret's gone all right,' the Vice-Commander muttered, latching on to a point I had noticed and hoped no one else had. 'But it's not lost: *they*'ve got it now. They've got it and we haven't.'

'They've got the metal as well!' came a louder voice from the other end of the table, I think it was the Shaman's. 'Know what that means? It means they can make as much blond iron as they like. Cover themselves from head to foot in the stuff, while we're left with nothing but rusty old soup-plates and bits of leather. If they do attack, we're done for, I tell you, we're crows' meat!'

I had to think quickly and speak even quicker, because remarks like these in the mouth of a Shaman can soon lead to panic. 'Nonsense!' I countered in my loudest, bossiest, Nurse-in-a-temper tone. 'Cowards' talk! Crow Mount has metal, but it has no Miners to mine it. And without Miners, there's no getting a mountain to part with its treasures. I know, because I've watched. Mule-bones may know the secret of *working* the iron once it's out of the ground, but he doesn't know the secret of *finding* it. Only the Miners know that. And the Miners are not going to pass on their secret in a hurry, of that you may be sure. Not to Mulebones, not to the Regent, not to anyone who until yesterday was their mortal enemy. On that count at least we are safe.'

I clung to this certainty all day, like a sick person to a charm: I'm no good at pretending, and I wouldn't have been able to calm everyone down the way I did, unless I had thought I was speaking the truth about the Miners' secret. But the longer the day grew, the weaker the certainty became, until it faded into something more like a hope, and finally just the shadow of one. I kept remembering things; things about Muley; things that made my hands go clammy and my throat flutter as if there was a moth trapped inside. The flash in his eyes, that evening by the camp-fire, when the Master Diggers were talking about their work. The night-time prying and spying down the mineshafts. His fascination for the Miners' machinery. The questions, the notes, the little models he had made of each machine. 'Playthings' for Dola? Of course not, they had been 'learnthings' for himself. Muley, with whom all things were possible, even foreign languages and invisible tables and the transport of unborn babies, had been studying the mining process in all its details. Not for fun, not for curiosity, but because he knew, even then, he was going to need the knowledge for his own twisted ends.

It wasn't until evening, however, when I went in to say goodnight to Eaglet, that my fear went the full circle and became a certainty again. And when it did I forgot Eaglet entirely, and forgot myself as well, and like a madwoman or a victim of the falling sickness I put my head in my hands and began to shake and shake and shake, unable to stop until the violence of the shakes shook me back to something like reason again. Because I was certain now of the worst.

Eaglet had been crying, I could tell from the streaks on his face: not much washing had gone on in the Regent's part of the castle, and the tear-tracks were as clear as wheel marks.

I asked him why he was so sad: it wasn't as if the Regent or Muley had ever been particularly close to him.

'No, it's not them, it's my suit of armour,' he said. 'They had no right to take it. What do they want it for anyway? None of them can wear it: they're too old and big and have too many arms. It's not fair, they should have left it for me.'

I had been wondering about the disappearance of the suit myself, ever since morning, and had come to the conclusion that it had been taken for melting. Which was a comforting thought, because it meant I was right and the Regent and Muley did indeed foresee a shortage of iron at Crow Mount. I explained this now to Eaglet, hoping he too would see the comforting side.

He listened carefully, his blue eyes wide and dry, but when I had finished explaining the tears welled up again and he shook his head. 'No,' he said, 'that's not the reason. They took it because they're mean and didn't want me to have it. Muley doesn't need spare iron for melting: he can find all the iron he wants. All the iron in the world if he wants.'

My shaking hadn't begun yet, there was no reason, but Eaglet's words troubled me and there was already the trace of a wobble in my voice when I spoke. 'C-c-can he?' I asked. 'All the iron in the world? How?'

'With his stone, of course,' Eaglet said carelessly, as if he was saying 'with his fingers' or 'with a trowel'. 'With his magic stone. The one he keeps in the pouch on his belt and never shows to anyone.'

'Never *shows* to anyone?' I must have said this fiercely and startled him (my voice, as you've probably noticed, often plays tricks on me when I am nervous), because I saw Eaglet flinch, and the tears which were brimming in his eyes, started to roll down his cheeks. 'Never *shows* to anyone? How come *you* saw it then? Eh? How come *you* saw it? Eaglet, tell me no fibs, or I'll . . . I'll . . .'

Eaglet was crying properly now. 'It's not a fib,' he sobbed. 'It's true! I saw the stone once when I was very little. I went into Muley's room without knocking and I saw him using it – playing with it – getting it to do its work. He was so cross when he looked up and noticed me, I pretended I hadn't seen anything; but I had. I'd heard him chuckling and muttering too in Miner language, "Ciappa fer! Ciappa fer!" and telling himself how clever the stone was and how rich it would make him. It was a smooth grey pebbly sort of stone with magic inside it, and when you ran it over a pan of metal shavings, the way Muley did, it picked up all the iron ones as if it was sucking them, and they stuck to it, and it got all furry and spikey till it looked like a big grey chestnut. It's true, I swear. You could find iron anywhere with that stone. Anyone could. Even a blind man. Even in the dark.'

There was a pause, and then a cry – mine? Eaglet's? I couldn't tell – and I heard Eaglet, as if from a long distance, calling my name, 'Mother!

Mother! *Mother!* What's wrong? What have I said wrong?'

But I was elsewhere by then, and couldn't answer. I was back at Crow Mount, all those years ago, listening to the words of the Miner Chief as he refused to describe the lost stone to me: 'No hints, Princess, no tip-offs: you'll recognize it all right when you see it.' (Well, I hadn't seen it and probably never would now, but I had recognized it beyond a doubt. Not a jewel stone, no, not even one as fine as the Raietta, but something *far* more precious: a magic iron-detector.) I was watching the Chief prod Hubert in the chest with his hammer and accuse him – the old 'Greylocks' – of stealing the Miners' tools. I was standing by the window with Tilly on the morning of the same day, looking down on the Miners as they went about their search: 'They're always losing bits and pieces of their gear,' she was saying, 'I've never known workers so careless of their tools.' I was in the courtyard of Fànes on the day of our return, listening while the Shaman trotted out his rhymes: 'We found a hammer underneath, A pick, a knife without a sheath.' (The missing tools: not mislaid, not filched by Hubert for re-selling, but deliberately stolen by Muley, like the stone itself, and then placed on the scene of the crime to make us think – no, not to make us think, to make us accept *without* thinking – that the Miners were the culprits.) I was in the hall of Crow Mount the night of my parents' murder, watching Muley as – gently, deftly, like a shepherd with his flock – he pointed our silly sheepy heads in just that direction. 'Grit and hammer spell a Miner to me . . .' 'What if the Miners were dissatisfied with the deal they had made with the King . . .?' 'What if they crept into the King and Queen's bedroom and poured poison in their mouths . . .?' 'I don't want to stir up trouble between our peoples . . .'

Liar! Bronze-faced, cleft-tongued liar! To stir up trouble between Fanes and Miners had been his aim from the start. And how well he had succeeded in his plan. He had been shifting us around for years now as if we were pieces on a chequer-board. And we, dumb and bone-headed like chequer-pieces, had carried out his every move. Blame! and we had blamed each other, Hate! and we had hated, Fight! and we had fought. How he must have laughed at us behind his snow-coloured, schemer's eyes. How he must have despised us. And I who had looked on him all along as a dear and trusted friend! (I was wrong about this last bit, incidentally, because Muley didn't despise people, or laugh at them, or feel anything about them at all: he simply used them, like you would a bucket or a wooden spoon.)

The most dreadful memory of all, however, and the one that started up the shaking, was the feel of Muley's hand in mine as he held it to comfort me.

Theft and Treachery

The hand had been ice-cold; like the Commander's; like that of someone who had been out in the storm for a long, long time and had only just come in. The truth of the matter struck me like a thunderbolt: Muley had been to Fànes and back that night, and even I in my stupidity knew now what he had done there.

CHAPTER SEVENTEEN

The Pledge

couldn't sleep a wink that night for cold. The touch of Muley's hand seemed to have gone from my memory into my body and spread to all my limbs, so that not even Lois's fur and my marten cloak combined were thick enough to warm me.

Snow was on the way, and this was good and bad at the same time. Good, because it meant we were safe from attack for the whole winter long and had time to prepare ourselves for whatever troubles lay ahead in the spring. Bad, because it meant that if I was to have a meeting with the Miners (and I must, I *must*, I would have no peace until I did), I had to be very quick about it.

The meeting, as I feared it would, proved extremely difficult to arrange. My first two dispatches to Mill Brook, sent via the Duranns, came back unopened, with angry war-crosses scrawled all over them; and on the third attempt our carrier was greeted with a hail of red-hot coals, one of which nearly singed her left eyebrow off. If it hadn't been for Nurse's brother, who by dint of bribery finally convinced one of his old dealer pals to smuggle a message through for us concealed in his leggings, I doubt we'd ever have managed to make contact at all.

At last, though, and just in time before the weather broke, an agreement of sorts was reached, and on what turned out to be the very last fine day of that danger-ridden autumn I found myself setting out from Fànes for the requested get-together with the new Chief of the Miners. (Whoever he or she was: I had no idea who had taken the place of my poor little misunderstood, beheaded friend.)

I was alone, save for Lois, who I had insisted on bringing, and Eaglet, whom the Miners, for some reason I was none too happy about, had insisted I bring. Save for Lois with his nails, we were all three of us unarmed. The only hard object we had brought with us, and not as a weapon but as a peace-offering, was the Raietta, tucked into a little tie-on bag at my waist.

We had received instructions and we followed them, down to the last crabbed, smudgy letter of the Miners' note. Not only unarmed, we were also bare-headed and cloakless, and we kept to the middle of the road as we'd been asked to, and left space between us, and didn't once turn round to see if we were being shadowed. When we reached the frozen waterfall, where the first envoy was to have been posted according to the agreement but wasn't, Eaglet and I dismounted and tied our ponies to the rings that are set in the ice for this purpose, and Lois straightened up from his running position, and then we all three sat down with folded arms (Eaglet couldn't really fold his, but still, he did his best) and waited for the Miners, wherever they were, to make the first move.

'Yrrr!' I shivered as we waited, 'I hate this place. I wonder why they chose it for our meeting. I'd have much preferred Mill Brook, smoke and all.'

Lois smiled and made a slight gesture of his head towards the top of the waterfall. 'They chose it because it's a good look-out post,' he said softly. 'See? There, behind the second ripple where the flat bit is? There's someone watching.'

So there was. I had seen right, then, when as a child I'd spotted that pair of squinty black eyes staring out at me from behind the ice. And acted right too when I had decided to go no further: this was very definitely a spot where intruders were not welcome.

Like I had then, I felt a sudden urge to turn back, only of course it was too late. 'We aren't walking into a trap, are we?' I half mouthed, half whispered to Lois over Eaglet's head.

'We could be,' he whispered in reply. 'But that's the whole point. You said it yourself, trust's got to begin somewhere.'

'They won't . . .' and I glanced down at Eaglet, unwilling to put my thoughts in words, 'pull any tricks?'

Lois shook his head firmly, calming me a little. 'Not nasty ones, no. They'll drive a hard deal if they can: Miners do nothing for nothing, the valley folk say you can't even get a fart out of them for free, but they won't do us any real harm, not once they know the truth.'

Eaglet giggled, as he always did when farts were mentioned. Unlike Lois and me, I could see he considered the outing a great adventure and was enjoying himself no end. Before I could stop him he lifted his head and looked straight into the peering eyes behind the ice and gave a happy wave. 'Ooh, hoo!' he shouted. 'Here we are, Miner Spy! Down here! Look!'

He meant well, but it was a tactless way to greet an arch-arch-enemy after years of bitter conflict, and the guard, when he left his post and came down to meet us, looked very cross and stuffy. He bound our eyes roughly, Eaglet's first, and then gave us a piece of rope to hold as a guide-line. 'Follow me,' he said – no titles, no pleases, just the gruff command – 'and mind your steps. The going's rocky and we've a long way to go.'

In the meanwhile we had been joined by other

The Pledge

Miners, some of whom had probably been following us along the route, but there was no talking among them and it was hard to tell how many they were. From the sound of their steps I'd have said three, but Lois told me later he had picked out seven different smells all told – none of them very wholesome.

We climbed for what seemed ages, but there again, silence and darkness play tricks with time and it was probably only a smallish slice of a sundial, had you been able to measure it. The Miners led us a roundabout way too, to confuse us; even I, who have scant sense of direction, could tell that. For most of the journey, except for the first part which was slippery, the ground underfoot was dry and the air dank, so although we were travelling up and up, we were also, with respect to the mountain, travelling in and in. Steeper and steeper and deeper and deeper.

Just as I was beginning to get really fed up with our journey (because it's horrid walking in these conditions: blindfolded and at the mercy of people who would like to see you dead), the dank smell changed, and the tilt of the pathway changed, and after a few more paces forward and then several downward the silence began to change too, and in its place you could hear the sound of crackling and fidgeting and the whispering of voices. First several, then many. Then, mingled with the whispers and eventually smothering them entirely, there came a furious sort of hissing sound: our welcome from our Miner hosts.

Unceremoniously the rope was jerked from our hands and the blindfolds were stripped off, and we found ourselves in a high-vaulted, dark-walled space lit by a fire in the centre and a smoke-hole far above it through which a single ray of murky grey light filtered down, fighting for admittance (and losing, so it seemed) against the smoke. In the resulting glow-cum-gloom I could see dozens, perhaps scores of Miner people, sitting on the floor with their legs crossed.

'Pssssh!' they spat at us, wiggling the upturned soles of their misshapen feet in an unmistakably hostile way. 'Psscchh! Fanes! Yeeaaccch! Bleaaah!'

To this pretty accompaniment we were half led, half pushed round the outer fringes of the fire and into the presence of the Miner Chief, who was sitting on the opposite side of the blaze in a raised chair of rather grand design – much too big for him.

He was so like the old Chief I had known that for a moment I thought it *was* him, come back to life again, but Miners weather badly and I soon realized it must be a son: a man, presumably, of my own age or thereabouts.

He wasn't hissing along with the others, he was polite enough to restrain, but his face was twisted into a sneer such as I have never seen.

'State your business, woman!' he rapped out

without preamble. 'And be quick about it. I guarantee your safety but not for long. My people are not dogs, that I can muzzle when the urge to strike becomes too strong!'

Oh, my word! Talk about putting visitors at their ease! I don't know how I managed to find my voice at all in those nerve-racking circumstances, let alone launch into the long, complicated story that I had to tell, but somehow I must have got started and somehow I must have continued and won my listeners' ears, because gradually the hissing died down and the Chief's face lost its sneer and began to wear a frown instead – first puzzled, then troubled, then simply sad.

When I got to the recent happenings, however, the sneer came back again with a vengeance. 'So you're in a pickle, my fine Princess,' he said when I had finished telling him about the Regent's betrayal and the stealing of our armour. 'That's the long and the short of it. You're in a pickle up to your pretty white neck and now you come grovelling to us – to your bitterest and most deeply wronged enemies – for help. It was all a mistake, you say – all a terrible, tragic mistake.' (His voice went a bit squeaky and affected here, and I think he thought he was imitating mine.) 'The seeds of mistrust were planted between us, through no fault of our own, and now we must sweep them away and begin afresh. Well,' (in his own voice again) 'let me tell you something, Alexa of Fànes: it is too darn late for fresh beginnings! Those seeds of mistrust, as you call them, have grown into huge great trees – into thickets, into forests – of mistrust, and no amount of sweeping can clear them away now. Your story is heart-rending, it would wring tears from a turnip, but personally I don't believe a word of it! Not one teenzy, dainty, lying little word!'

But he did, I knew he did, or was beginning to. I could tell from the way he was nibbling at his finger ends: the Miners always did that, I remembered, when they were edgy.

'It doesn't matter what you believe,' I said, taking a step towards the chair and looking him level in the eye, the way I had done with his father all those years ago (you never knew: frankness had worked then, it might work now). 'The facts will speak for themselves soon enough. And I've not come here to grovel, either, or ask your help, I've come to warn you: we Fanes may be in a pickle all right, but you are in a pickle too. Every bit as sticky and every bit as hot. It's the *gold* Mulebones wants, can't you see? It's the gold you've got stored away in your famous treasure-trove of Aurona. He's been after it from the start. The quarrel, the war, the iron, the weapons – these were just means towards an end: his real goal is Aurona and it's only a question of time before he and the Regent find out its whereabouts and launch their attack. Fresh beginnings! Who spoke of beginnings? You must have misheard me. This is the *end*, my Lord of the Miners: the end for my people and the end for yours as well, and there's precious little, so far as I can see, we can do to avert it.'

You could have heard a daisy drop, the gathering had grown so quiet and still. In fact, not daisies because there weren't any, but I could hear the noise of the Miner Chief's teeth cutting through his cuticles, followed by a soft little 'paff' as he spat them aside.

Gingerly he climbed out of the chair and lowered himself onto the platform, where he remained standing on tip-toe so as not to lose face by losing height. It was a first, minute signal of civility. 'Why *should* I believe you?' he muttered, half to himself. 'How can I? What have you ever done to merit my trust except behead my parents and persecute my folk?'

'The Princess didn't give the order for the beheadings,' Lois said quietly, speaking for the first time. 'I swear. If you can't believe her, believe a Salvan. Salvans live underground like you do; we share the same customs, we share the same Gods.'

'Worms live underground,' the Chief said shortly. 'So do wraiths.'

'The Princess didn't give the order,' Lois repeated, still very calm and reasonable. 'The revenge party acted without orders of any kind. And she sent the heads back, remember? Even though she thought your father had killed her parents, she sent his head back for burial. Was that the action of a dishonourable ruler?'

'Mmmmn,' said the Chief. His eyes were so slitty they were hard to read but I had a feeling he was coming round. 'Mmmmn. Honour. Honour is what my father went by, and look where it got him: I prefer to use my nut.' And with his fingertips he rapped his little dark nobbly head, which indeed, being shaven, did have something of a nut about it. 'The cases are two: either you have come here in good faith, like you say you have, or in bad. If you have come in good faith, so much the better; you may depart from here unharmed and rest assured that whatever the new year brings to Fànes it will not bring hostility from us. Help you haven't asked for, and wouldn't get it if you had, but you won't have hindrance either. I think that is fair enough, don't you?'

I nodded: after all the blood spilt between us it was fair enough.

'If, on the other hand,' he went on, 'as I suspect and *continue* to suspect in spite of all the jaw, you come here in *bad* faith, then you may still depart unharmed, but not before you have listened to this. You have brought your Salvan with you, Alexa the Slippery. And don't think I don't know why. You have brought your Salvan, because your Salvan,' and he gave a funny little mock bow in Lois's direction, 'can find his way back here now. Isn't that right?'

Lois, taken by surprise, began to mumble some kind of answer but the Chief didn't wait to hear it. 'Save your breath for your tracking, marmot!' he barked. 'Do you take me for a fool? You want to come back, at least you think you do, because this is the hall of Aurona in which we are now standing. You know that as well as I do, so spare me the flummery and take those silly gapes off your faces!'

Easier said than done. I wasn't just surprised I was astonished, and Eaglet was so excited he began to squeak.

'Although to do you justice,' the Miner Chief went on, glaring hard at Eaglet in a vain attempt to silence him, 'perhaps you *are* a little surprised. You thought, with the ploy of the secret meeting, I would lead you somewhere near to Aurona, somewhere in the right direction, isn't that so? Some place from which the Salvan could start his sniffing? Instead I bring you right into the heart of our treasury. Why is this, you will ask yourselves? Because I am even dimmer than you think? No, my foxy Fanes and snakey Salvan, because I am brighter than you think. I *want* you to learn where we keep our treasure, see? Yes, I want you to know the whereabouts of our famous store of jewels and gold. So! Look around! Feast your eyes on it! And then go and tell your friends at

Crow Mount and come back and steal it whenever you like!'

'I don't see any gold,' Eaglet said puzzledly. He was too young to understand sarcasm.

'No more do I,' said the Miner Chief, and gave a shrill, bitter-sounding laugh. 'But then my eyes were never that good.' And still chuckling he clambered back on his chair and began scratching at the back of it, pressing his nose to the wood. 'Must be some here, though. This is my throne – used to be covered with the stuff. Must be some somewhere.'

And he had accused *us* of flummery, if you please. Lois had urged me not to, seeing that our position was so delicate, but I began to lose patience. 'Basta!' I rapped out in the Miners' own language, which means 'Enough'. 'We have come in good faith, or we wouldn't have come at all: however bad your eyesight, surely you ought to be able to see that. And what's all this fuss anyway about the missing gold? I don't understand. Do you mean to say you've lost it? That you've none left, not even a flake?'

The Chief glowered at me, but composed himself and stopped his antics on the chair. 'Not lost,' he said. 'Spent.'

'Spent on the war?'

'Nah,' he drawled: sarcasm was evidently a favourite device of his, and to be honest my silly question deserved it. 'On chitterlings. Of course we spent it on the war. D'you think the Cajutes did our fighting for us because they liked the look of our faces? No, they did it because we paid them – through our blinking noses. Paid and paid and paid until there was nothing left.'

'I'm sorry,' I said lamely. And I was: it was sad by any reckoning to think that the magnificent realm of Aurona we had heard so much about was reduced to this: just an ugly, smoky cave with nothing in it but a bare wooden throne and a bonfire. However, as I lost no time in pointing out to the Chief, it only went to show how wickedly we had been tricked, both of us, into waging this cruel and needless war in the first place, and how important it was we forget the past and try to be friends.

The little man listened, his expression still sour. 'Friends!' he snorted when I had finished. 'Easy for you Fanes, with your full coffers and your full stomachs, to talk of friendship, but as for me I'd like to see you back it up with something a bit more solid. A nice pledge of friendship, for example, from you to us – how about that? Just to put your purse where your tongue is, so to speak?'

A pledge? Ah, so we were coming to the bargaining phase, just as Lois had foreseen. 'Willingly,' I said quickly. Perhaps too quickly, because when you bargain you always ought to play for time. 'Only I'm afraid I haven't brought anything of value with me.' (This was untrue, of course, because I had the Raietta and the Raietta was priceless, but it is not good manners to say of any gift that you are about to make that it is valuable.)

My delicacy was lost on the Miner Chief, like a lace collar would be on a boar. The narrow eyes moved sideways until they came to rest, sharp as a couple of glinting knife-blades, on Eaglet. 'Not a some*thing* maybe,' he agreed, 'but you've brought some*body* very precious. We saw to that. Make a very good pledge, he would, this chirpy little son of yours here, can't really think of a better.'

For one dreadful moment I feared the worst and felt panic rising inside me, fast and unstoppable as froth on beer: so *that* was why the Miners had made me bring Eaglet, they wanted to kidnap him and use him as a hostage. How could I have been so foolish as not to see this earlier? How could I have been so doltishly, oafishly foolish?

This time, however, it was me who was being distrustful. The Chief was looking to his own advantage all right, but it was a long-term and slightly different advantage he had in mind.

'Tch, tch, Princess,' he tutted before I could say anything, reading my panic and waving a fore-finger in my face the way Zeno used to when I fluffed my lessons. 'No hasty conclusions. I was merely extending an invitation to the little prince, that's all; merely thinking how nice it would be for my daughter to have some companionship of her

own age this winter. You haven't met my daughter, have you? Well, I'd like you to, I'd like you
both to.'

And with a quick bird-like movement he
swivelled round on his chair and plucked at the
head of the courtier sitting closest to him, catching
a tuft of the man's hair between finger and thumb.
'Fetch the Princess Sommavida from her nursery,
Kal,' he ordered. 'Tell her we've got a surprise for
her.'

The courtier got to his feet with very bad grace
and disappeared into the shadows, rubbing his
head. I reckoned on a wait while he went about
his errand, imagining the palace of Aurona even in
its decline to be huge and rambling and full of
corridors, but the nursery couldn't have been more
than a few paces away, if that, because within an
eye-blink the man was back, holding by the hand
an incredibly dirty and incredibly ugly little female
Miner, whose age, had we not been told it already,
it would have been impossible to judge. From her
size she could have been two, from her shape and
wrinkly skin she could have been a hundred and
two, and from the eyes that looked out from the
skin − lustrous, guarded, watching everything,
missing nothing − she could have been Dola's
age, slap in her prime.

I had no intention of leaving Eaglet in the
company of this unappetizing infant crone for an
afternoon, let alone a whole winter, but the trouble

was, seeing the way the Chief had masked his request, it was very difficult to refuse without causing offence. And the Chief was counting just on this.

I won't take you through the 'But no's, and the 'You are too kind's, and the 'We couldn't possibly's, with which I tried to wriggle my way out of the deadlock. The discussion, which was quite long enough already, seemed as if it would never stop, and in fact we didn't get back to the Waterfall and our poor, tethered horses until almost nightfall.

When we did get back, however, Eaglet was still with us, thank the stars, and the terms we had beaten out between us, the Miner Chief and I, were as follows: 1) The Raietta passed from the Fanes to the Miners for ever, as a gift, free and unrequested. 2) The Fanes, in the person of their Ruler, undertook to recover the Miners' magic stone for them at the earliest opportunity and to return it without delay to its rightful owners. 3) As a gesture of goodwill and in hopes of forging closer ties between the two said peoples (the Miner Chief wanted mention made of an engagement, but I managed to squash that one) the Prince of All the Fanes, named Eaglet, currently six-and-a-half, would spend not this winter and not any winter, but the first fortnight of every spring, until his thirteenth birthday, with the Miners, in whichever of their dwellings they happened to be living in at the time. 4) As a reciprocal gesture of goodwill the

The Pledge

Miners, when they came to fetch the Eagle Prince for his first stay, would deliver to the Fanes a red stone, no bigger than a plum but no smaller than a cherry, to replace the Raietta in the crown.

'I'm sorry, my lovekin,' I murmured into Eaglet's ear as I carried him up to bed. 'I'm so sorry for what I've let you in for, but I had no choice.'

'I know,' he said, although I wonder if he did. And then he added in his cheerful voice of always, 'Don't worry, mother. I don't mind spending time with that little Floor-mop, as you call her; I thought she looked rather sweet.'

CHAPTER EIGHTEEN

A Winter Wedding

hate remembering things connected with Muley, but he taught me so much and shared so much of my life it is hard not to sometimes.

Once, for example, he told me about a man who was obliged as a punishment to live with a sword hanging over his head, attached to a thin bit of thread that might break at any moment. I thought that was a terrible state of affairs and said so, but Muley put me right about this: it was no sort of punishment at all, he said; we all lived, every instant of our lives, with a sword like that poised over our heads, the important thing was just never to look up and notice it.

I don't know whether I followed this advice deliberately that last winter at Fànes, or whether the Sun God saw to it to hide the sword from me as a gift, but I know that despite everything we were happy. All of us.

After all what was lacking? Time? But you can't stow time away in the storehouse with the prunes even if you want to, so where was the difference? We had food, we had firewood, we had our friends and families around us and everyone we loved. (And nobody that we didn't, which made a nice change, at least for me.) And we had so much to do one way and another, what with strengthening our defences and making wedding preparations, that our heads were mostly down anyway, bent over our work.

When the solstice came, or when the Shaman lost patience with his measuring rods and *decided* it had come, Dolasilla and Ey de Net were married. It was more than a marriage, though, because a married Queen, no matter what her age, is no longer an Infant Queen but a real one, so I suppose you could say it was a Coming-to-Power cere-mony or a Beginning-of-the-Reign ceremony, almost a second coronation. That, anyway, is how we celebrated it: in grand style, as only Fanes know how.

Sometimes, as Nurse and Sonia and Tilly and I busied ourselves about the preparations – making clothes, weaving garlands, experimenting with new dishes and polishing and decorating pretty well everything in sight – I wondered if we were right to spend so much time on just a feast, a passing event, when we had so many other, graver jobs to do. But I was pretty sure then, and *quite* sure now, that we made the best choice. More arrows, more shields, more sling-stones – these things wouldn't have made much difference to the final outcome; at most they would have prolonged the fight by the sifting of a sandglass, maybe two. Whereas, even though it was all over so quickly, there is a sense in which the last great party of the Fanes in honour of their last great Queen is with us still. With all of us, I mean, even those who only live on, with the memory, inside my head, or those who simply hear me tell about it.

The ceremony on Plan de Corones all those years ago was splendid, like all bright and new things are, but the wedding of Dolasilla and Ey de Net, in the banqueting hall of Fànes, amongst the flares and the festoons and the dark, rich swags of leaves and fruits and berries on the walls, was so beautiful it took your breath away. It didn't do to look too closely – we had few materials to work with and everything was put together with spit, as Nurse kept telling everyone, but somehow, just because you knew how fragile it was, the overall effect was magical, heart-catching, far lovelier than I can make it sound in words. It didn't matter either that there were fewer people, and no sunshine, and that the sound of our music, instead of pouring out over the peaks and valleys, remained trapped in the rafters for us alone to hear: it was, everyone agreed, a Fanish feast anyway, and the best and finest ever held.

As soon as winter was over and the roads were clear – maybe even a little sooner, because they are expert travellers and can sneak their way through the narrowest of tracks – the Miners came for Eaglet, as had been agreed on in the treaty.

They came in a dog-cart, four of them, wrapped up in skins to the eyebrows: from a distance you could hardly tell which were the animals and which the passengers.

We smiled and made them welcome, and kept smiling to the moment of send-off for Eaglet's sake, but as soon as the sledge had left the courtyard our faces, almost of one accord, became serious. It was as if, in his little rucksack, along with his clean clothes and the dress Tilly had made as a present for the Floor-mop, Eaglet had packed up the carefree atmosphere that had blanketed us all winter and taken it away with him.

I hated losing him but I was glad to see him go: Muley, who knew everything, would waste no time looking for Aurona now that the gold was no longer there, and I reckoned therefore that Eaglet was safer with the Miners for the time being than he would be with us.

And I reckoned right. Only a few days later the first group of Wanderers arrived at the gates and brought us various bits of news, each worse than

the last, and worse still when put together. Mining
and metal working on a large scale had been going
on at Crow Mount all winter: the slopes round the
castle had been so scorched by the fires and
trampled by the workers that the snow hadn't
even settled there, and the crag had stuck out
dark and bare for everyone for leagues around to
see. Like a bad tooth, the Wanderers said. What
was more, an outcast who lived in a cave nearby
(could it have been Luna's brother, I wondered,
thanking me for his dinners?) had reported the
presence of Cajutes among the workers. Not just a
few but many, and not prisoners either from the
looks of them but free men and women going
about their job with a will. And now that the roads
were free, the Wanderers themselves had seen still
more Cajutes, on the move, heading in the Crow
Mount direction. A bunch of Peleghetes too in
fighting gear, and a straggle of Latrones: it looked
as if some kind of gathering was taking place at the
Regent's court, but what it was in aid of it was too
early for them to tell.

Not for me, it wasn't. For me it was late. Like in
the game Sonia used to play with Eaglet, when she
would cut up an apple for him in funny-shaped
pieces and try to get him to put it together again,
the last little missing bit of Muley's plan slid into
place, leaving me to see the smooth, perfect shape
of the whole. And like in the game, which was
hard at the beginning but got easier and easier as

you went along, the last bit was the simplest of all to fit.

Only fools waste time looking for things that are hidden; clever people make sure first that they know where to look. That is what Muley had said to me once, and that is what Muley had done. Not knowing where the Miners' gold was stored, and knowing that he would never find it just by searching, he had worked things so that the gold left its hiding place almost of its own accord and shifted to another spot, the whereabouts of which he knew exactly: the Cajutes' coffers in the Cajutes' castle.

'Then he and the Regent will attack the Cajutes now, not us,' said the Commander, trying to sound hopeful, when we discussed the matter at our next (and last) meeting of Council. 'That'll learn 'em all right. Even if they're clad in blond iron from head to foot, those Crow Mount milksops are no match for the Cajutes; they'll be ripped to chaff.'

But I had to disillusion him. No, I told him sadly – told everyone sadly. Muley's plan was simpler than that, and tidier. There was no need for him and the Regent to take the gold from the Cajutes by force: they could do it, indeed already had done it if the Wanderers' reports were correct, by means of a simple business deal. One treasure for another. Yellow gold for blond iron. They had sold the secret of the blond iron to the Cajutes in exchange for the Aurona gold, and in doing so they had sold Fànes too.

'And everyone inside it!' yelped the Shaman, never at his best in a crisis.

'And everyone who *chooses* to remain inside it,' I corrected him. 'Those who don't can leave now for the high pastures with the children, and no shame attached.'

In fact, apart from Nurse who was in charge of the group that was leaving, and the one guard assigned her (both of whom were under orders and had no choice in the matter), none of my brave, loyal companions took advantage of this offer; I had hardly expected that they would. Tragically, very few benefited from it either, even among the children, seeing that on the day of battle, when the sounds of fighting reached them in their hiding-place, all those above toddling age gave their two keepers the slip and came homing back to Fànes to lend a hand in the defence. Poor lost neenies, battle-happy from the cradle, how I wish they hadn't; how I wish I'd been able to send them away to the Miners, like Eaglet, for safe keeping.

And yet, even then, in the tail-end period of waiting, when the sword swung so low that a dwarf upside down couldn't fail to see it, it seems to me now we were still happy in a queasy sort of way. I remember those last evenings that we spent together, Dola, Lois, Ey de Net and I, stretched out in front of the fire as in my childhood, with the dogs lolling in our midst, snoring and whiffling in their dreams, and a bowl of walnuts set between us, and a flask of wine, left over from my father's store, from which we took turns to sip. We didn't talk much: our days were so busy that we scarcely had the breath, but the knowledge of time running out on us acted as a kind of seasoning, like salt on food, so that those few words we said and those few gestures we made seemed packed with special meanings – messages we wanted to give each other but daren't. You can't say, 'I love you' to someone you love on the eve of a disaster, you can't say, 'I have always loved you, even when I thought I didn't,' or 'Forgive me,' or (as I wanted to say to Ey de Net), 'I think I am beginning to love you too'; and yet with our 'Who wants another swig?' and 'How's the arrow situation going?' and 'Wonder if Eaglet's getting on all right' and 'D'you remember that day Nurse found a hen in her piss-pot?' that was more or less what we said.

Or perhaps this is me being sentimental in my old age. Perhaps we really bickered like starlings: Lois urging me to call on his kinsfolk for help before it was too late, and me wanting for Lujanta's sake to keep the Salvans out of it and refusing; and Dola backing me up, and Ey de Net siding with Lois just because they were men. And perhaps the dogs stank, and there *was* no wine, only beer and Schniappa. But anyway, whether happy or crabby or a bit of both, there were so few evenings left that it hardly mattered. On the morning of the Feast of

Frenzy – the day that is set aside for mad people, and a very fitting day it was too – long before cock-crow and long before even the faintest paling of dawn, we were woken by the noises we had been expecting for days now and had heard in our dreams all winter. At least I had. First a baying sound, like wolves only bolder, shriller. Then a kind of slow rhythmic chanting, broken now and then by war-gongs and the stomping of feet, Wheyla, wheyla! Oing! Clomp, clomp, clomp! No trouble guessing what it meant: our enemies were assembling outside the walls and miming in dance the things that, all going well for them, they would shortly do to us for real.

I stood at the window with Lois by my side, peering out into the darkness, and as the light began to spread we saw what appeared to be an endless, borderless crowd of warriors, encircling the castle completely and reaching as far as the eye could see. It was like being surrounded by a flood, only of people, not water. Ey de Net, when he joined us, swore that there were no Duranns amongst them, and I hope for his sake he was right, but otherwise, apart from the Miners and the Cadubrenes who had both kept their promises and stayed away, there was not a tribe or a branch of a tribe that had not turned out in full force to take part in the storming of Fànes – all of them coated like birch trees in the brightest and blondest iron I had ever seen. Cajutes by the hundred; broad-faced, slant-eyed Peleghetes whose women fight with their babies on their backs; lakeside Lastojeres and mountain Lastojeres; Ampezzani, Trusani; Latrones, scruffy as always in spite of their gleaming new gear. And behind them all, on the fringe where the warrior-flood ended and the trees began, the Crow Mount contingent, recognizable by its black wing-shaped standard and the huge, unmistakable, top-heavy figure of the Regent on horseback. Poor horse.

'I didn't think he'd have the guts to show his traitor's face,' Lois said, and spat in the direction of the standard.

'He doesn't need any guts today,' Ey de Net murmured in a little rag of a voice. 'If he stays placed where he is, it'll all be over by the time his turn comes.'

'Tchah,' scoffed Lois. He was the only one of us, I think, who wasn't frightened, or whose fright had already stiffened into rage. 'We'll see about that. No battle is ever over before it's fought, and no place is so safe that the Bear God can't fetch a man from it if he chooses.' And so saying he turned his back on the window with a scornful shrug and went off to get my fighting gear for me from the Armoury.

CHAPTER NINETEEN

The Storming of Fànes

The last time I had dressed for battle it had been with Dola, on the day of the Prince and the poppies. Today, because of the vow Dola had made then, I expected to dress alone, but no sooner had I started strapping on my bits and pieces than Dola joined me, her arms full of dark clumsy metal plates – the best our smiths had been able to turn out.

I knew at once what she intended to do, and although it was to me like the coming-true of a nightmare, there was nothing I could do or say to stop her.

'They must see me there, you see,' she explained, almost impatiently, as she began girding herself in the armour. 'I can't fight, on account of the vow, but I can't stay out of the fight either, or

223

the soldiers would lose heart. Don't look at me like that, you know that if you were Queen of the Fanes you would do the same.'

Would I? At her age, with so much life still to live? Just stand there in the fray to be shot at, in order to give other people courage? No, I don't think I would have stood that kind of test: Dola was younger than me and her body was smaller, not yet fully grown, but inside she was much, much stronger. It terrified me, that strength of hers, the way it always had: weak people, like reedy plants, can bend in the face of a storm and pop up afterwards, but the strong ones fall like trees.

'I won't be in any great danger,' she said lightly, sensing my terror and trying to calm it before it showed. 'Ey de Net will be there, he'll look after me. He's used to shielding both of us.' Then, whistling ever so softly so as to fill the silence she buckled on her last plates and began helping me with mine.

When we were dressed and ready she called Sonia, just like she had that other morning, and together the three of us arranged the new crown on her head, with the red stone in it that the Miners had brought. (More cherry-size than plum-size, but that was only to be expected.) We tied it on the outside of the helmet this time, with no hair showing, and the effect was quite different – harsh, falcon-like, foreign. So foreign that when she finally went out on the ramparts to take her place among the soldiers there, they had trouble recognizing her.

'Who's this ugly black creature giving us orders?' they shouted in dismay. 'Where's Queen Dolasilla? We want our Queen Dolasilla!'

But when they did recognize her a great cheer went up, because word had been going round that Dolasilla would not take part in the battle, and now everyone could see that this was not true.

That cheer is one of the last clear, separate things I remember. Very shortly afterwards, almost as if they had heard it and taken it for a war-cry, our enemies launched their attack, and from that moment I was plunged, like a snail in the soup, into a small, hot, swirling world from which there was no exit, no view, nothing except a succession of immediate dangers needing all my energy to foil them. Block that arm, it has a lifted sword in it. Rush to that spot, they're spilling in like ants. Drag that girl away from the oil-runnel: she is useless there, something's happened to her eyes. Get down, Alexa, you fool. Duck your head. Get up again. Run for cover. Find a new sword, yours has had it. There, grab that one, the owner's got no use for it now. Godsbones! What was that? Never mind, didn't do much damage; bind it up with this piece of flag here and get back to business. That soldier needs you, so does . . . No, too late, go back to the other. Make sure first he's one of ours. Slowly now, watch it! There, in you go, hard as you can, no pity. What's pity? Thud. Cronk. Gurgle. Give another hack. (Still no thrill inside me, but no fog either this time, just a thick pair of Warrior's Blinkers, keeping me to my horrid task.)

I didn't see the Commander fall, I didn't see Lois, I didn't even see Dola, though the terrible howl the soldiers gave to mark her end must have penetrated my ears without my realizing it, because afterwards, when the sun went down and the fighting stopped and the King of the Cajutes rode up to the gate to dictate his terms to us before scuttling off smartly with his troops into the dusk, I needed no telling of this particular piece of news.

Their stories, or the end of each of their stories, I had to discover for myself from the way I found them on the field. Lois's was simple. He lay a good distance away, on the very edge of the wood, and it was clear from the wounds on his body, which were so many and close together you couldn't even count them, that he had been set on by a great number of opponents. Not far from him lay the Regent, dead as drag-meat in spite of the blond-iron casing which covered him from top to toe. A single rift was visible in the armour, at throat level, where the helmet stopped and the breast-plate began, and it was here, evidently, that Lois had got him. Recently too, because the blood of both was still liquid. Even through my tears I could see what had happened: the Regent and his followers had kept out of the danger area all day long, just as

Ey de Net said they would, and Lois, when he had realized this, had burrowed or clawed or fought his way through the enemy forces to this spot, bringing the danger area with him. He must have known he could fell only the one victim, if that, so he had felled the Regent, and then submitted to the Crow Mount knives. (No, not submitted, Lois would never submit to anything, but you know what I mean.)

The Commander, like a lot of our best soldiers, had fallen defending the main entrance, and it was thanks to the press of their bodies blocking the doorway, giving the impression of a resistance that had long since ceased to be, that the King of the Cajutes drew back his troops that evening into the woods instead of entering his conquered domain and taking possession on the spot. (I think he was frightened about being caught in the open when the dark fell and being set on by wraiths, and I can't say I blame him. As I said before, I'm not sure I believe all the things that are told about the Unready Dead – how they can't find rest, and have to traipse around the world until their time is ripe, latching onto people for warmth and scaring the daylights out of them and so forth – but if they *do* exist, then that night there must have been a lot of them around in the vale of Fànes.)

Tilly was on the stairs which led to the grain-hatch, with the Kitchen Salvans and a dozen or so of our young domestic workers – all girls, none of them seasoned fighters – in another horrible tangle which spelt of struggle to prevent entry, but here it was the enemy who seemed to have prevailed. The bodies, Tilly's in particular, bore mud marks, as if they had been trampled on by dirty feet, and the hatch swung open and a ladder stood directly underneath, still propped against the wall. (Poor Tilly, I can scarcely think of anything she would have hated more than to die like this, covered with mud marks – she who so liked everything to be clean.)

Dola and Ey de Net lay where they had been at the outset: on the ramparts, their bodies on top of each other at what Zeno called wrytangles, forming a cross. People don't usually look pretty in death, and they were no exception, but they didn't look ugly either. Not to me. They looked young, almost like children, and they looked healthy, as if they weren't really dead at all but pretending. Both had died of arrow-wounds to the chest. Ey de Net, who had been hit first, looked as if he lingered, at least long enough to try and remove the arrow from his wound, but Dola, I was relieved to see, seemed to have died instantly. Her helmet was off, but Ey de Net must have removed it for her, or else one of the soldiers, because her hands were still under her, clasping tight her unstrung bow.

When I get to this part of my story I usually have to stop, because even now the memory, when it really comes back to me, not in words but in images and feelings and sounds and colours, is so sad it makes my voice crack. 'How you must have *hated* that foul old Mulebones,' my listeners sympathize, while they wait for me to go on again. 'How you must have cursed him to the Gods. What did you wish on him? What would you have done to him if he had been there? Would you have torn him apart like Lois did the Regent? Would you have set on him and caved his snowy eyes out? Bet you would, bet you would! And serve him right, and serve him right!'

Again the truth is hard to explain to them, little and candid as they are. Muley had won, and got his gold – all to himself now, presumably, for the Regent would hardly be needing it, the state he was in – and through his fault and his greed I had lost everything: my parents first, and now my daughter, my lover, my friends and kinsfolk, my happiness, my home, my entire world. I should have hated the creature all right, bitterer than anyone ever hated an enemy, but somehow I couldn't. Because to hate him was to think of him, and to think of him was to hold him in my head alongside Dola and Lois and Ey de Net and the others, and this I didn't want to do, for their sakes. For their sakes I needed my head to stay clean.

All this, however, is very difficult to explain to a plain-minded audience who like people in stories to behave the way they do. So I usually say yes, I would have torn Mulebones apart like Lois did the Regent, and wait for the cheering to die down before going on to the part my listeners love best: the Mill – or the Morin as it is called in their language – of the Salvans.

CHAPTER TWENTY

Morin de Salvans

The King of the Cajutes had granted us a day and a night for the burying of our dead, after which, he said, he would be back for our surrender and the handing over of the keys. Any resistance, any holding back, and we would be threaded through our middles on a rope, like so many beads, and strung out over the courtyard for the crows to feed on.

A day and a night – two nights counting the battle-night – would have been ample time if we had been even half the number that the King of the Cajutes imagined, or even that I myself imagined before I started counting. But the sad, almost unbelievable truth of the matter was that there were only eight of us left. Eight unhappy, unlucky survivors – one of them a child – to bury an entire population. There was me, there was my dear, darling Sonia, who never slept through another winter afterwards, her dreams were so bad; there were four young Fane warriors, two men, two women, these last both with serious arm wounds; there was the child – the only one of the brave but foolhardy band that had slipped Nurse's vigilance and returned; and lastly there was the old, blind head-stableman-that-was, who had hidden himself away in the half-empty ice-pits with the dogs, not being able to take part in the fighting, and had saved himself that way, at the relatively cheap price of a cold in the head.

You might think – I thought so for a moment myself, and the thought was like honey it was so sweet – that the best way out of such a dire situation was simply to join Dola and Lois and the others in the underworld without delay and have done with it. I would be going there shortly anyway – we all would: surrender meant slavery, and slavery under the Cajutes was unthinkable. But then I saw the old head-stableman rolling up his sleeves and getting down to work (he was doing everything wrong, of course, lining up all the wrong bodies and putting the enemy ones in with ours when he should have been placing them separate, for removal), and I was ashamed. What sort of a welcome would our companions get from the Bear God when they reached his lair, if they hadn't even been announced? No, I couldn't desert them by joining them, not until I had given them a proper send-off.

And then, if I needed any more convincing, there came a sound of shouting and jeering from a distance, and in the no-man's land between us and the enemy encampments in the woods, Nurse suddenly appeared, hedged about by a group of armed Latrones, with her clutch of toddlers – five of them – piled into a wheelbarrow. There was no sign of our Fanish guard; Nurse told me afterwards that he had been killed, trying to defend them, the moment their hiding place had been discovered.

'Look what the cat brought in!' the soldiers shouted in their thick Latrone accent, chivvying Nurse forward and causing the barrow almost to tip. 'Thought you was safe up there, eh, y'old witch, but you warn't. We can smell rubbish a mile off, we can, and rubbish goes where rubbish belongs. Shoor! Scarper! Into the swill-bin with the lot of you!'

We had difficulty hauling her and the children in to safety, because the entrance was still blocked, and the ladder leading to the grain hatch had already been drawn up and hacked to pieces. Eventually we used a basket on a rope for the children, and just the rope for Nurse. The enemy soldiers did nothing, either to hinder or help, but stood underneath and made rude comments about Nurse's underside. Normally I would have found this offensive, and Nurse even more so, but we were all so tired and miserable we were past caring. And anyway, as Nurse pointed out, there couldn't have been much of a spectacle as it was nearly pitch dark by then and she had her canvas bloomers on.

After the return of the toddlers there was naturally no further question of taking the swift way out that night, or even thinking about it. They needed care, they needed food, they needed sleep. We all of us, whether we wanted it or not, needed sleep. So finally, when we had fed the babies and the dogs, and covered up our dead the best we could to keep them from the birds, we lay down on a pile of straw in the stables – none of us wanted somehow to enter our ravaged homestead – and slept like dead people ourselves. Huddled up close to each other for comfort and warmth.

All next day we worked and made plans. The work wasn't very cheerful work, consisting as it did in holding funeral after funeral for each of our slain companions – all hurried, all makeshift, none of them as they really should be – and the plans weren't very cheerful plans. Being the only writer left, that day I must have written out a mile of messages to the Bear God, introducing his new guests to him, begging that he treat them well, and explaining in each case that the shabby send-off we gave them had nothing to do with lack of love. 'On earth this person was good and brave and precious,' I wrote, time after time (even for poor Tecla, who wasn't all that good, and for the

Shaman who wasn't all that brave). 'Please excuse travelling dress, Please welcome, Please do not turn away.' In Dola's case I added 'beautiful' between 'brave' and 'precious' and put 'Queen' instead of 'person'; in Lois's case I was tempted to add an extra something special too, but in the end, knowing how he hated fuss, I left the message as it was.

By the time night came we had finished all this sad business as best we could, although our only solution for a resting-place for our companions being the ice-pits, and our only idea of closure being some lengths of linen laid on top of the pits like an extra-thin coverlet of snow, our best wasn't really very good.

Meanwhile, between funerals, the grown-ups amongst us had come to the following decision: that night, as soon as the little ones had got off to sleep, we would set free the donkey, the ponies, the horses and the rest of the livestock and let them take their chances in the outside world. You never knew, with a bit of luck some of them might get through the lines, others might find good homes with the enemy soldiers: the Cajutes in particular were dotty about horses. (And dotty about chickens too, though in a different way.) Next we would dig a deep hole in the ground somewhere safe and secret and bury the two important emblems of our vanished kingdom to prevent them from falling into enemy hands: Dolasilla's crown with the red stone in it, and the heavy, chamois-horned head-dress I had so disliked wearing. Thirdly we would carry as much straw as we could into the stable where we were presently camped, bank it up round us in a circle, and douse it with what oil we had left, ready for firing.

At this point but not before, any grown person who wished to could take their chances along with the animals and make a run for it. Because however low the chances, and however high the risks, it was only fair that each man and each woman choose their own way of leaving. Those of us who remained would sit down together in the ring of straw with the sleeping children and drink all the flasks of liquor we could lay our hands on – emptying the rest (for I was blowed if we would leave any for the invaders). And finally, when the liquor had done its work but before its work wore off again, we would free ourselves in the only way left to us. Dogs first, then babies, then oldies, then middlings, then – last of all – me, whose job it would be to set a candle to the oil-soaked straw before joining the others.

Quite a programme. I don't think any of us found it as daunting as it sounds, though, because at the point we had reached, the Bear God's refuge, cramped and dank as it probably was, seemed far more inviting than the Sun God's realm above ground where for us the sun no longer shone. The only regret I remember having myself was that I should die without having passed on the Great Secret to Eaglet, as my father had bidden me, and as I had promised him to do. But quite honestly it didn't worry me much: I tended to agree with my mother that the whole business of the Salvan alliance had been grossly overrated. Ah yes, and speaking of Salvans, I regretted never having known my other daughter.

Anyway, we carried the programme out as planned, step by step, and sip by sip. When the nest of straw was completed and there was no more heavy work to do, the four young Fanes – as I had thought they would, and as I most likely would have done myself in their position – chose the outside route to liberty. They dressed themselves in some old herdsmen's smocks we found hanging in the tack-room, so as to appear less conspicuous, and covered their blond hair in rags, and smeared their faces with dust, and with just a silent farewell hug to us and a kiss to the sleeping children, they made off into the darkness. Under my breath I wished them luck. By which I meant a clean, quick end, like ours.

By this time I must have been, not extremely but fairly seriously, drunk. I could feel my hold on myself slipping – could imagine myself falling asleep and not doing any of the terrible and necessary things I had to do, but waking up instead, in a kind of addle-headed relief, to find that the enemy had broken into the castle and that it was too late.

I told Nurse and the old stableman to remain with the babies, and together with Sonia and the dogs I went out into the cold night air to see if I couldn't sober up a bit. Not much, mind you, or I would slip the other way, but a just bit.

The night was bright and silvery and still, and the thought went through my mind that if I stayed in the world long enough I might possibly, one day, one night, find it beautfiul again. I chased the thought away, because that wasn't slipping, it was sliding headlong.

'No noises,' said Sonia, swivelling her ears around the way Salvans do when they are listening hard. 'Good. Perhaps they've got through after all. Perhaps,' and she coughed to hide the eagerness in her voice, 'perhaps we could try following them.'

You try, I was just about to urge her (hoping that she would, because I trusted myself to be resolute with the others when it came to it, even the tinies, but with Sonia I was afraid my hand would tremble), when I saw her stiffen. The dogs too. 'Hear that?' she whispered. 'Over there, near the wine cellars. There's someone moving, there's something going on. Wait a blink . . .' and she moved closer to the entrance of the cellars and dropped to her knees and put her ear to the ground. 'Yes, there's someone down there, I can hear them scrabbling. Who can it be? What can it be? Oh, Alexa, help! I'm scared!'

I could hear nothing, and as for being scared –
what had we to be frightened of now for goodness'
sake? Wraiths? Bogeys? Pookas? Giant woodlice,
coming out of the ground in search of supper?

'If we want to find out, we'd better go down
and see,' I told her, quite unflustered, in fact glad of
the chance to gain some extra time, and went to
fetch a candle.

Once we reached the bottom of the cellar stairs,
however, where the scrabbling noises could be
heard clearly, and where a part of the floor, close to
our feet, appeared to be moving ever so slightly, as
if it was a sand-bog or a piece of wormy cheese, I
was no longer quite so calm. The dogs stood beside
us snarling and shivering, fixing their eyes on the
moving portion of ground, which I could now see
was taking on a raised, square shape, like a hidden
trap-door that someone is trying to open; one of
them, which was strange, began thumping its tail.
The candle in my hand wobbled so hard that
everything seemed to move, not only the floor,
and I reached out to grasp Sonia's hand, which was
wobbling too, and together all of us watched,
riveted, as the trap-door creaked slowly open
and first a long set of nails, then a hand attached
to them, then an arm, then a shoulder and a neck
and a head, and finally a whole earthy person,
surfaced from the hole in the floor and got slowly
to its feet in front of us.

Mothers are meant to know their young by a

special sense – look at sheep, the way they pick out their lambs in all that muddle, and mares the way they find their foals in the thickest of herds – but I don't think I did, not straight away. My heart leapt, it is true, but first because I thought it was Lois, come back to life again, and then, when some of the dust came off and I saw it was a girl not a man, because I thought it was Dola.

She looked like both, you see. Amazing gift from whichever god I have to thank for her: she looked like both. Her hair, which I had imagined dark, was as blonde as Dola's, and she was tall and straight and slim like her and had the same way of carrying her head – proud, verging on the snooty. Her nose was Dola's too; by which I suppose I mean that it was mine, only slightly smaller. But her eyes and mouth were Lois's, kind and wide and smiley, with nothing hidden in them at all, except, possibly, a tiny blot of sadness, too small and private for most people to notice. Her feet I couldn't see that night, the light was too faint, but I had already realized from her digging abilities that hands and nails had also come to her from her father's side. (What would the Regent have made of that, I wonder? I know what Lois's mother would have said, though: she would have said, Not all harm comes to harm us, or, Every cloud has a copper lining – meaning that things didn't turn out so badly after all.)

And she, Lujanta? Did she feel anything then? She says not, but I remember her standing there in the candlelight as she shook herself free of earth, and staring at me almost in fright, as if I was the one who had made the surprise appearance, not her. So, yes, I think she must have felt something too, only of course she was not in a position to know what.

Also there was very little time for feeling anything except the need for haste.

Sonia, who from terror seemed to have switched to high excitement without any interval at all, swivelled her ears again and hissed. 'Ssss! They're stirring!' she whispered. 'Our enemies are on the move again, I can hear the drums!'

At this Lujanta moved her hair aside to listen too, and it was then that I noticed – not without a slight shock, I will admit – another gift from Lois: a pair of long, furry, pointed Salvan ears. Ah well, could have been worse, could have been the teeth!

'How many are you?' she asked in Salvan, ignoring me and speaking directly to Sonia. 'Are there just you two, or are there any more?'

'There's a litter of us,' I put in quickly (there are no words for numbers in Salvan, from three you go to clutch, and then litter, and then just herd). 'Upstairs, in the stables. Sleeping.'

'Ah,' Lujanta said. You could tell she was surprised to hear a Fane speak her language so well, but like Lois she was sparing with her words and made no comment on it. 'Wake them then, and fetch them. Quick. Now.'

I didn't tarry, not even to nod. I snatched the

candle and, moving so fast I almost quenched it, rushed up the stairs and ran to the stables to do as I was bid.

We had some trouble with the babies, Nurse went into such a flap she kept dropping them and couldn't seem to realize why it was we couldn't use the wheelbarrow, but eventually, carrying one each and me slinging the fifth one on my back like a Peleghete, we managed to ready ourselves for flight. Above ground the noise of the enemy drums could be heard quite clearly: there was very little time, and none at all for wasting.

As we left the stables I threw the candle on the oil-soaked straw, and we made our way to the cellars in a darkness broken by the growing light of the blaze. Burn, Fànes, burn, I said to my home as if it was a person; cover our tracks for us and give our enemies a warmer welcome than they ever bargained for.

But Fànes could not cover our tracks for us entirely: this much became apparent when, one by one, or rather, two by two on account of the babies in our arms, we began to make our escape down the mouth of the tunnel.

Sonia went first with the littlest and lightest baby: being a Salvan, Lujanta said she could rely on her to follow the right trail and not lead us all by mistake into one of the underground pits or rivers, of which there were several along the route. Next, minus baby but with the dogs on leashes to take care of instead, went the child. Then Nurse with her bundle. Then, in theory at least, the old stableman with his, and me with mine, and Lujanta bringing up the rear with hers. However, when it came to this point I saw Lujanta (or rather felt her, for the darkness was so deep you couldn't see a thing) pass her baby on to the stableman with a rapid, shoving gesture, as if she'd had second thoughts about carrying it, and heard his startled murmur of protest – 'No, ma'am, no. That's not right, can't let you do that!' – and realized in a flash what she was up to: she was going to stay behind to cover the trap-door with earth again and prevent the invaders from discovering our escape route. And she was right, someone had to do it, or we would have them on us in no time.

But not her, not my strange, beautiful gift-daughter I had just found. I don't quite remember what happened next, whether I lunged out at Lujanta and tried to push her down the hole by force, or whether I too tried to deposit my baby first in the laden arms of the stableman, only to meet with a refusal, or whether it was the other way round and he tried to foist his pair on me, but I know that there was a great tussle between the three of us, and a lot of screaming from the poor tossed-around infants, and a lot of angry words that weren't angry at all, but desperate, and then suddenly a silence in which only the old man's voice could be heard, pleading, begging, craving for me to listen to him. 'It's been vegetables all these years, Highness, don't you see? All these years, and I've never been able to do anything to be proud of, except trim the veg and wash it and clean it. I'm old, I'm blind, I had to hide away like a coward during the battle, I couldn't even do much afterwards to help – give us this one chance, please, of a little tag-end of glory. I'll do things properly this time, I promise.'

I began to argue, explaining how it was my duty as a ruler to protect all members of the tribe, young or old, but he cut me short with a furious kind of whistling noise: his kitchen knife slicing the air under my nose. 'I'll kill meself, Highness,' he warned. ''Less you leave this instant, I'll kill the lot of us, starting with the babes!'

It came in a funny disguise, what with knife and fury, but thinking back on it this threat of the old stableman's was probably the most generous gift I have ever been given, containing as it did Lulu and the future and life itself, wrapped up in one hastily put-together package. I doubt he would have touched a hair of any of us really, but this time I didn't quibble.

'Bless you,' I said, and felt out in the darkness for his old work-stained hand and kissed it. 'Bless every bone in your body.'

'Gerrout!' he replied, snatching his hand away. And passing over to Lujanta the baby still in his possession, so that she now had one and me two, he pushed us roughly down the mouth of the tunnel and slammed shut the trap-door over our heads.

As we set off down the tunnel to join the others, however, he opened the flap just a hand's width and called out in a very different voice – his real one now, 'Bless you, Highness, and bless Fànes. Tell the little Eagle Prince he will come back here one day as King. Tell him, remember.'

Yes, I thought, and one day snow will fall upwards and the moon turn square. 'I will tell him,' I called back. 'I will remember.' And then I increased my pace, for already the sound of Lujanta's footsteps on the sandy floor was growing fainter.

'Where are you taking us?' I shouted after her as I went. Not that it really mattered as long as it was away from Fànes.

'Morin,' her voice reached me with a funny echoey sound to it: Mo-o-orin. 'Morin de Salvans.'

And where on earth was that? 'And where on earth is that?' I yelled back.

'Nowhere,' she replied. 'It's *under* earth. It's the safest place in the world, you wait and see.'

It had better be, I thought to myself: if any of us are to come out of this jam alive to tell the tale, it had certainly better be. And went on following.